The DEVOURING

by R S Cunningham

First Published in 2025 by R S Cunningham
With Russell-Alexander Publishing Ltd
Edited by Russell-Alexander Publishing Ltd

Cover Design by **Lucian Tumani**

https://luciantumani.myportfolio.com

ISBN: 978-1-0369-2976-3

Contents

Dedication

To the friends and family whose unwavering support, advice and patience made this possible.

You know who you are.

Prologue

The Doctor and I appraise each other across the room. Rats scramble in my abdomen. I clench my fists. I smile brightly, trying to appear non-threatening.

Judging by the look on the Doctor's face, it isn't working.

The Doctor glances at the door.

My stomach drops. *Please don't call the orderlies to take me away before we even begin,* I beg silently.

It's taken me so long to regain my access to these therapy sessions. I force myself to calm down, breathing slowly through my nose.

"How long has it been since we last spoke?" the Doctor asks in a cool tone.

"You'll have to tell me that, Doctor Neilly." My voice cracks as I look around for water.

Ever attentive, the Doctor stands up and passes me a hard plastic cup with a straw, ensuring I grip it properly with my gnarled, twisted hands. The water is cold and delicious, and I sip greedily while the Doctor sits and scans my file.

"I'm pleased that the experimental medication is working better than expected. Your periods of lucidity are more frequent, and you're more lucid than usual during those periods. There's such an improvement that it's been recommended that we restart our sessions. How do you feel about that?"

The Doctor stares at me, eyebrows raised. I smile blankly but I don't answer.

We both know the experimental drug trial results are horseshit. My file is full of lies.

"If I remember correctly," the Doctor pauses and leans towards me before continuing in a clipped tone, "our last few sessions, many years ago before they had to stop, were very upsetting for you."

Upsetting? That's quite the understatement.

I keep smiling brightly, but my cheeks are starting to burn.

No need to be afraid, Doctor.

"Nothing wrong with your memory, Doctor. No sign of you being admitted to my loony ward, eh?"

I laugh feebly and pause to choose my words carefully. I'm on thin ice and we both know it. It took me a long time to get back here.

Careful. Mustn't blow it now.

I sit on my hands to stop them shaking.

Doctor Neilly leans back and glances towards the door again. In panic, I start to ramble.

"Just because the sessions can be upsetting, Doctor, doesn't mean I don't want to meet with you. I want to talk about the past. I want to remember. The loss of my hands, my poor eyesight, not recognising faces or voices, no bladder control, no bowel control; none of those symptoms compares to memory loss. It's like, like my existence is being wiped out, and I can't stop it or fight it because, well, because I'm the one erasing myself. I can't accept that I'm beyond help, destined to become a husk, a shell. Please, give me a chance. I really do want to be here."

Moments pass as the Doctor regards me coolly.

I hold my breath.

The Doctor leans forward and lifts a notepad and pen. I exhale. Yes!

"Will you be retelling the same memory as before?" The Doctor asks.

I try to sound confident. "Er, yes. Yes, I will." I sound pathetic.

"And why should I listen to it?" The Doctor's tone is cold and professional now; any forced warmth is gone.

"Because, because that's when my grip on reality started to disappear. It's when I lost all understanding of what's real and what isn't. It's the last thing I remember clearly."

The Doctor sighs deeply and looks at me sternly. "You know I'll have to cut this short if it gets too much. Don't you?"

If I get *upset* again.

"I understand, Doctor Neilly. I'll be fine. I promise."

"Hmph. We'll see. Very well. Begin."

I take a deep breath and start at the beginning.

Chapter 1

The Gathering, 18:30

I stare at the yellow door. It is exactly the same shade of yellow as the Harland & Wolff cranes that loom behind me on the Belfast skyline. Of course it fucking is! The owner, Joanna, never failed to remind me that she was very proud to be Belfast born and bred. God knows why.

I open the plastic bag in my hand and peer at its contents: an eight-pound bottle of Spanish red wine with the yellow reduced-price sticker still on it and a packet of slimy green olives.

Oh, I really don't want to be here.

I had taken two buses across town from my West Belfast high-rise as my car was on the blink again. The thought of doing the journey in reverse wasn't appealing, but neither was knocking the yellow door.

I scan the street. It's a riot of colour as the auburn autumn leaves almost completely cover the pavement. Unlike my neighbourhood which was mostly covered in litter and dog shit.

Maybe no one saw me arrive. Decision made! I'll text and make an excuse.

I turn and begin to walk back down the driveway, fishing in my pocket for my battered iPhone 4.

"Hello there!" Dammit! One of Joanna's friends is striding noisily up the path towards me.

"Oh, you must be the cleaner! Joanna said you were joining us. I'm Eleanor. No answer, eh?" she shouts unnecessarily. No chance of sneaking anywhere with this loudmouth nearby.

"Yeah, that's me. I don't believe we've met before." Awkwardly, I extend a gloved hand. Do women shake hands at these events?

Eleanor ignores me, turning to bang her pudgy fist loudly on the yellow door. She's wearing large, garish costume rings with bees, flowers, and art deco designs on each finger. I pull my hand back. "The Cleaner" it is then! Maybe I'll get a name badge with "The Cleaner" on it, like when I work at hotel conventions.

The yellow door swings open theatrically and Joanna appears, as always, looking fantastic in a bright blue and pink printed maxi dress with a matching blue silk scarf tied around her long blonde hair. I try not to smirk as she pauses for a second, allowing us time to admire her outfit. There are hugs, compliments, toothy laughter and air kissing. Between Joanna and Eleanor. Not me.

"Come on, get in. The rest are already devouring the good stuff."

We enter the hall. It's freezing. Colder inside than outside. Who doesn't put the heating on when they're expecting company? Eleanor and Joanna walk down the hall together, chatting loudly. I feel the radiator. It's blazing hot. Maybe Joanna flicked it on too late.

Reluctantly, I follow the waft of Jo Malone perfume down the wide hallway into a large open-plan kitchen/dining/living room bigger than my entire flat, with very high ceilings. The room smells amazing. I pause for a moment, breathing deeply to take it all in.

Pots are bubbling on the Aga, and the large breakfast bar is laden with more food than I could ever fit on my tiny kitchen counters. My eyes roam over it greedily; Ciabatta, olives, pâtés, cheeses and crackers, vol au vents, carrot cake, trifle, cocktail sausages, chicken skewers and dips - all served on what I know is locally sourced, artisan pottery. I know because Joanna insisted on giving me the artist's card, so I too could spend twenty-five pounds on a clay bowl large enough for ten peanuts.

My slimy supermarket olives will be jeered off this table. Maybe I'll bin them or shove them in my tights for later.

Joanna comes over and wrestles me out of my coat. I note the large log burner is ablaze, but a chill is in the air here, too.

"Help yourself, but save room for dinner," Joanna says with a warm smile before disappearing with my coat through a side door to a utility room that's larger than most people's kitchens. She returns moments later to find me standing exactly where she left me, hugging my plastic bag like a life raft.

"How rude of me. I forgot you don't know anyone. Shall I introduce you? Is that for me?" She talks without drawing breath, all smiles and arm rubs. We have a minor tussle before I capitulate and pass her the plastic bag. She thanks me and sets it aside before leading me into the cavernous room.

The first person we come to is loudmouth Eleanor again. Now that she has her coat off, I can see she's wearing a maroon velvet jumpsuit that accentuates her enormous bosom and belly, along with a lot of chunky gold necklaces and brooches.

"Oh, we met already!" She squeals when she sees me. "Isn't this your cleaner?" She asks, looking past me to Joanna.

"Well, we certainly don't call her 'The Cleaner,' Eleanor!" Joanna admonishes with a fake scowl. She turns to me, smiling expectantly, and I smile back.

A beat passes. I do, of course, realise she is hoping I'll introduce myself. But something in me twists, and I don't feel like throwing her a lifeline. In fairness, Joanna did try a few times but couldn't quite master pronouncing my name.

I've been her cleaner for the past two years, and she's managed to get by without using my name the entire time. Instead, lots of "Hey You" comments are thrown my way, or she just calls me by my initial "M," pronounced "Em." Now that we are with company, this annoys me more than it does when we're alone, not least because Joanna thinks she is a wonderful woman to work for and is completely oblivious as to how I really feel about her.

"So, M," Joanna says, a little too loudly, "this is Eleanor, who I was telling you about. She's a dear old friend of mine and, of course, a local business owner. Eleanor, meet M."

I turn to Eleanor. Feeling self-conscious around so many posh Belfast accents, if that's not an oxymoron, I try to soften the harshness of my Southern Irish accent as best I can. "The Cat's Miaow, I believe?"

"Oh, you know it! Yes, that's the one! The delicatessen on the corner of Sunnyside Street, off the Ormeau Road," Eleanor says, beaming with pride. "I've been there a few years now. Do you ever call in?"

Of course, I know it. You couldn't miss it. It looks like Elton John's and Liberace's interior decorators got together to open a shop and tried to outdo each other with oversized, gilded mirrors, arty paintings of saggy boobs, stuffed neon animals and so many plants you can't see from one side of the shop to the other.

The Cat's Miaow is the sort of beautifully decorated, overpriced shop/cafe/haberdashery that I avoid at all costs for fear of being charged twenty quid for a small square of cheese or embarrassing myself by mistakenly trying to buy an ornament that's part of the decor.

My friend, Orla, went in once in a shameless attempt to act middle-class with new friends from her gym. The sourdough she ordered had such a tough crust it dislodged one of her fillings! She moaned for weeks afterwards about how a bit of bread and jam cost her over two hundred pounds when she factored in the subsequent trips to the dentist.

I smiled falsely, "Oh yes. It's lovely there! Didn't it expand recently?" A cloud passes over Eleanor's face, and Joanna clears her throat. Christ on a bike, what have I said now?

"I put a few small tables and chairs on the pavement over the summer. Well! When I tell you the local council are dicks about permits, you have no idea!" Eleanor bellows at me. I imagine it was the Mums who could only pass by the shop by pushing their prams onto one of the busiest commuter roads in Belfast who were being the 'dicks.' A couple of the other women turn to see who is shouting, and Joanna takes the opportunity to leave Eleanor and steer me over to them.

"These two are my very oldest friends. We met on our first day at big school, if you can believe it! M, this is Lindsay-Anne, and this is Sarah. Ladies, this is M." Joanna beams at the women with obvious affection.

Lindsay-Anne and I have met before when she was over for coffee with Joanna, and I was trying to clean invisibly around them. Not easy with a Henry Hoover, I can tell you.

"Call me LA; everyone else does," Lindsay-Anne says warmly.

"Nice to meet you bo...," I begin, but they have already started talking over me.

"Is this everyone who's coming, JoJo?" asks Sarah, speaking with her mouth full. "When will we get started?"

"Would you ever have some patience!" Joanna waves her hands towards the breakfast bar. "Give people a chance to get a bite to eat."

"Who are we waiting for?" asks LA, before popping a mini vol au vent into her mouth.

"Umm..." Joanna scans the room. "Let's see, you three, Ameera and Eleanor are here so far. So, we're just waiting for Lydia."

LA and Sarah roll their eyes and groan theatrically.

"You didn't give her the *actual* time to arrive, did you?" LA asks.

"Um, well." Joanna squirms. "It's not easy to give one person different info when we're all on the same bloody WhatsApp group, LA. You know?"

Sarah and LA groan again.

"Is Lydia notorious for being late, then?" I ask awkwardly, trying to join in the conversation.

"Late?" scoffs Sarah. "Late is half an hour to an hour after the meeting time. Lydia has been known to arrive at a dinner booked for seven at half bloody nine!" They all laugh.

"God, do you remember that?" Joanna says between laughs, "AND she was raging we'd all eaten!"

"Is she bitching about me?" The women flinch. A severe-looking lady has sidled up behind Joanna without us noticing. Oh yeah, Joanna doesn't lock her door most of the time. Something that always surprises me, given how much her house screams *money*. Ironically, I always lock my flat, even though any would-be burglars would probably look around and leave me a tenner.

"Good God, it's a miracle! Ring the Vatican!" exclaims LA, flinging her arms in the air. "Unless you died horribly in a crash on the way over and joined us from beyond the veil?" she says in a mock spooky voice. I wonder how long she's been here and how much she's had to drink already? The women laugh, and the tension is diffused.

Joanna passes Lydia and me beautiful, handmade, green clay plates and gold napkins. Lydia, Sarah, Joanna and LA start making animated small talk that I'm almost, but not quite, included in while we stand around the breakfast bar.

As I smile and nod politely, holding my empty plate, I wonder again about my invitation here.

I clean at Joanna's house for three hours, twice a week. She pays well, and the work is manageable; she has just a few cats and hamsters as pets and no hairy dogs like some other clients.

About a month ago, Joanna made a point of sitting me down and telling me about a special night she was planning. She was having friends round for a 'Gathering,' and she explained that this would be a storytelling session which, apparently, is a very trendy thing to do. She and her guests would be "Raconteurs." I nodded knowledgeably to hurry her along but had to Google the word when I got home. It means storytellers, if you don't know. Admittedly, I should have guessed.

I asked Joanna if she wanted me to change my day to come and clean before the party, after, or both. But no. She was inviting me to come along! I didn't have to worry about telling a story, but I could come "for the experience."

Honestly, imagine inviting someone to a party at your house 'for the experience.' It's like Joanna can't hear how she sounds to other people. How is a house party an experience just because your friends are telling stories? They're hardly bloody celebrities. It's so typically Joanna to assume I'd gratefully give up my weekend to be here. Sure, what else would I be doing? I was entirely uncomfortable with the invitation and tried to decline politely many times. But she brought the subject up every time I was at her house, and it soon became impossible to say no. Joanna tends to get her way. So, here I am. A rapt and appreciative listener for this charming bunch of middle-class overachievers.

Sensing my discomfort, Joanna took the time to tell me about each of her guests while I cleaned and she hovered over me drinking a latte. I remember her telling me that LA is a renowned solicitor and a real crusader for disadvantaged women's rights. Apparently, she won an award recently for her pro bono work.

Subtly, I look at LA's outfit. Her navy dress looks expensive, made of thick material and cut to flatter her curves. I'm guessing she bought it from Whistles or Phase Eight. I can't even afford their stuff on sale. She has accessorised with discreet diamond jewellery and high-heeled, brown leather knee boots over patterned navy tights. She's pretty, with flawless make-up and blonde, highlighted hair that looks like it's just had a salon blow dry. She's single, without any kids, and she's reserved but not unfriendly looking.

In contrast, Sarah, who is make-up-free, has flat mousy brown hair, and is wearing navy jeans and a black polo neck jumper that must have been bought quite a few pizzas ago. Her polo is accentuated by a cheap-looking statement necklace that I recognise from M&S.

Joanna told me Sarah is a doctor in the Royal Maternity Hospital where there are too many pregnant women, not enough funding, and not enough doctors. Sarah has three kids under ten and is married to a "right useless bastard" apparently. No wonder her looks aren't a priority.

LA is nursing a glass of gin while Sarah has an enormous glass of red wine and the look of a woman on a mission to enjoy every minute away from those three kids and the aforementioned useless bastard.

I turn to eye up Lydia. Jesus! She looks positively angry. Her face is set in a scowl, lips pinched and pursed. I was surprised at Joanna's candour about Lydia when she was giving me the lowdown, describing her as "an acquired taste" and "not for everybody," which felt like an unnecessarily mean way to describe an old friend to someone who didn't know them. Joanna insisted, unconvincingly, that she liked Lydia, giving me the impression Lydia had been in the friend-group for so long, they couldn't cut her out - no matter how much they wanted to.

Lydia is wearing minimal make-up, white jeans, a badly fitted, pink linen shirt and a pair of tatty old trainers. Clearly, her appearance isn't a priority for her. You'd think she'd make a bit of an effort before coming here, especially as Joanna always looks like she's about to do a cover shoot for Hello! magazine.

I shouldn't be so bitchy. I swear I wasn't always so bitter, but I'm not sure that's true. I look down at my black and white print shirt dress, bought in a Next sale a few years ago, snagged black tights and battered black Chelsea boots. I should have at least polished my boots. But that would require being the sort of grown up who owns boot polish, which I'm not. Chin up, old girl. You're at least two stone lighter than both LA and Sarah. Ha! Oops. Once you start being bitchy, it's hard to stop.

I notice Lydia is listening to LA and Sarah with a disapproving expression. Sarah is animatedly holding court. Mid-story, I start to listen in.

"That is not true!!" Joanna interrupts Sarah loudly. "You are lying!"

"Swear to God!" Sarah shouts back at her, one hand raised, as if testifying in court. "Haunted vagina! That's what she said!"

LA roars with laughter beside her while Joanna stares, open-mouthed in theatrical surprise.

"What the fu..? Wait. How on earth does someone think their vagina is haunted?!" Joanna practically yells at Sarah.

Lydia turns to me and rolls her eyes, but I have taken the giggles too. What the hell?

"I'll tell you now." Sarah continues, laughing and waving her glass in the air. "So, she's single, and she doesn't drink. This is important to note. This is because she is, in her own words, 'a good God-fearing Christian and pillar of her church.' However, the same strange thing keeps happening to her.

Every night, she says her prayers and going to sleep. Sometimes, she wakes up the next day and realises two things. One, she is violently hungover, and two, there is a random guy in her bed. At this point, she cracks up, yelling and screaming at the poor guy, asking who he is and why he's in her house. The weird thing is that all the guys have the same explanation. They insist they met her out at a club where she was downing shots like it was her last night on earth and that she practically dragged them home for 'the ride of their life.'" Sarah explains, making air quotes for the last sentence.

"Ha!" hoots LA, drinking more of her gin. Even Lydia cracks a tight smile.

"So, the only explanation, and I mean *the only* explanation that makes sense to this God-fearing, Christian pillar of her community, who is now inconveniently and embarrassingly pregnant out of wedlock is...say it with me, ladies!" Sarah says in a loud, singsong voice, hands in the air like a conductor.

"Her vagina is haunted!!" chorus Joanna and LA.

"Exactly! Haunted by a horny ghost, apparently." Sarah continues. "I mean, I shouldn't mock. There's clearly some mental health stuff going on there. But honestly, best laugh I've had in ages. Oh! Oh! And I haven't even told you about the Church Elder yet! The horny aul toad has offered to 'treat her,'" more air quotes, "with a, and this is both a direct quote and the name of my upcoming side hustle on Etsy, 'a range of blessed dildos.'"

"Ah fuck off! You're just making this up now!" exclaims LA, laughing loudly.

Sarah raises her hand again. "Swear to God! It's been the talk of the Royal. I'm surprised it hasn't hit the Belfast Telegraph yet!"

I smile and nod as the women continue their loud discussion, taking the chance to look around the room.

Eleanor and Ameera have taken their seats at the dining table and are deep in conversation. I recognise Ameera; she's also a doctor who occasionally appears on local news broadcasts about the state of the NHS in Northern Ireland. Originally from Scotland but of Asian descent, she's tall and striking, with long black hair. She's wearing an expensive cerise silk shirt, along with tailored navy trousers and tasteful gold jewellery. Ameera is as lean as Eleanor is curvy, with her huge bosom bursting out of her jumpsuit.

The wood-burning stove is lit in front of the sofas over in the living area. Strings of gold fairy lights are wrapped around the windows, giving a cosy golden glow. I try not to roll my eyes. What is it with middle-class women and their obsession with fairy lights? Still, the room looks stylish and expensive while feeling homely and cosy. I wonder where Joanna's kids and husband are tonight.

The chatter carries on for a while as the old friends catch up. Unnoticed, I help myself to some of the food. It's as delicious as it looks, much nicer than what I buy in Iceland and Lidl. I wonder if it's from The Cat's Miaow? If so, was it free? I can't picture Eleanor doing anyone any favours. If not, it must've cost a fortune. No expense spared for Joanna's thirty plus 'girls.' And twenty-eight-year-old me, I guess.

I look around and realise Ameera has stopped speaking with Eleanor and is looking at me with something akin to pity. I smile brightly at her, but she flinches and looks away. Jesus, this is painful. She must also be wondering why I'm here.

No one has given me a drink yet, which isn't helping. I spy delicate wine glasses next to rows of wine bottles and chic pewter coolers on a nearby worktop. There's no sign of the bottle I bought. It'll probably be re-gifted to me at Christmas.

I sidle over and pour myself a large glass of Rosé, gulping half the glass at the first swig. It tastes expensive. Generously, I pour myself some more. I have no intention of doing this night sober.

Eleanor's voice rings out, "Right JoJo, are we getting started now or waiting until we've had dinner?"

There's also dinner? My eyes sweep sarcastically over the barely touched spread. I wish Orla was here. We'd have eye strain from the side-eye and eye rolls by the end of the evening. I should have asked for a plus-one.

Joanna jumps to her feet dramatically. "Oh, go on then. Let's get started, shall we? We have time for one before the Tom Kerridge Bombay potatoes are done." She checks the food in the Aga while the rest of us make our way over to the round dining table.

The table can seat eight but is set for seven. I sit with Ameera on my right and an empty chair on my left. Wine glasses are generously refilled. Joanna flicks off the ceiling lights before joining us, sitting to my left.

Thank God for the fairy lights!

The ladies laugh and giggle in the darkened room. There's a pleasant atmosphere of anticipation. Joanna taps her wine glass with a spoon, her face a picture of mock seriousness, which is greeted by more giggling and oohing as the ladies get comfortable. It's impossible not to appreciate Joanna's warmth and humour. For the first time this evening, I feel myself relaxing a little. The wine is definitely helping.

At Joanna's direction, everyone around the table links hands. Ameera and Joanna each squeeze my hands a little harder than is comfortable. Joanna leans forward, her wide-eyed face lit by candlelight, and she begins to speak in a husky voice as she makes eye contact dramatically with each woman in turn.

"We are gathered this night,

When the moon is bright

And the veil is thin

To tell our dark tales that reside within

We call forth the memories

That steal sleep and sanities

The dark deeds done to us

By that which cannot be explained by us

In turn we'll speak

Truth to seek

And light to find

In memories bleak"

The giggling has stopped now; replaced by nervous tension. My pulse quickens slightly. We look expectantly at each other.

"Been reading 'Wicca for Dummies' again, have ya love?" deadpans Lydia.

"You cheeky witch. I've been working on that all week!" retorts Joanna playfully.

"It took you a whole week to come up with that shite?" LA pipes up. Everyone roars with laughter, and the tension is broken. Ameera and Joanna release my hands. Joanna has a faux wounded expression as she jogs over to the dimmer switch to bring the lights up slightly.

"Right, before I burn the Jamie Oliver Chipotle Chilli altogether, who's going first?"

Suddenly nervous, I look around to see who'll volunteer. When Joanna asked me to come, she reassured me I wouldn't have to speak, but I feel panic starting to bubble, like I'm back in school, being asked to answer a question on a topic I haven't studied. Does everyone know I'm just here to listen?

Thankfully, Lindsay-Anne, or LA as I'll never be comfortable calling her, clears her throat to get our attention.

"I missed the last gathering, and my story has been on my mind lately," she begins quietly while absent-mindedly twirling a diamond earring. Is this the hot-shot lawyer I've heard about? Why does she look so nervous in front of her friends?

"Some of you have heard this, but some haven't, so I'll just start at the beginning. You may take that

Jamie Oliver chilli off the hob, Jo!" she says jokingly, but her voice is strained. She looks... sad.

Curious, I lift my glass and lean back in my seat.

LA swallows hard before she begins her story.

Chapter 2

LA's Story - 'Click'

~~~

LA: *I was surprised to get the invitation for tonight. Joanna used to be a demon for these Candlelit Suppers, as we like to call them to wind her up, but she hasn't thrown one in ages. I have hardly seen or heard from Joanna at all lately. Since her youngest sister, Ada, took sick, she's been off the radar, so I was surprised to hear she was organising another Gathering. Maybe she's trying to distract herself or cheer herself up. I wonder if this means Ada's prognosis has gotten better or worse. Last time I called Joanna to ask how Ada was doing, she was very vague and I didn't like to pry. I checked with Sarah and all she'd tell me was that A would remain in hospital for the foreseeable future.*

And why the hell did she invite her bloody cleaner?! She doesn't even know the poor woman's name. M-something or other. One of those pretentious overly Irish ones. Only Joanna could think the person who comes twice a week to clean her house would want to traipse back across town on a Saturday night to spend her weekend with her boss and her friends. As if the Jamie Oliver bloody chilli is enough of a draw! Fuck sakes, I barely wanted to come. It's bad enough having to put up
~~~

with Lydia thinking she's Yvette bloody Fielding, now we have to bare our souls in front of Joanna's flipping hired help! I rang Sarah for a moan and to suggest booking a restaurant in town somewhere instead, but she was having none of it.

"It's just one evening. We need to show support while Ada is so ill..." she said reasonably.

"Why can't we all go out for dinner and drinks like normal friends?" I retorted, unreasonably. Sarah didn't have an answer and hurried me off the phone with an excuse about her kids needing her.

I get that Joanna loves the chance to show off her house and her cooking skills, making enough food for twenty people for a party of seven. Sorry, a 'Gathering' of seven.

And the bloody ghost stories again! When I heard the cleaner was coming, I thought 'Great! She must have a new story for us.' Turns out she's only here to listen!

It's hard enough talking about what happened to me with friends, let alone strangers.

God help the poor woman. I bet Joanna hasn't even told her how dark these stories are; they're not for everyone.

Oh well, she seems to be hitting the wine, so that'll help her.

I've volunteered to go first, so then I can sit back and enjoy the food and drink for the rest of the evening.

~~~

"My story took place about ten years ago, in 2005. I wasn't long out of Uni, working for Campbell & Graham, and feeling like I could conquer the world with my shiny, new law degree.

My company had gorgeous new offices near the City Hall. I bussed it in every day and spent my lunches, on the rare days when I got a lunch hour, shopping for clothes I couldn't afford. We went for after-work drinks two or three times a week. I was making good money but always seemed to spend more than I earned. I was always broke and always out. I loved it. The work was hard, but the trainee lawyers always had such a laugh. I don't think I've ever enjoyed any job so much.

Anyway, this isn't a story about work, but it's important to note my frame of mind at the time. I HAD MADE IT! I wore LK Bennet dresses, Hobbs shoes, Jaeger coats, Anya Hindmarch handbags, all bought on sale of course, and was permanently doused in Chanel No. 5. I thought it would help me seem older. Even my tights were expensive; £20 a pair! What was I thinking? I had notions of myself.
~~~

There was a lot of homelessness in Belfast at the time. They concentrated around City Hall and Royal Avenue during the day to beg from office workers and tourists. Scurrying past them in my expensive outfits pricked my conscience. We often spoke about them in the office. "Poor guys," we would say with exaggerated sympathy. They probably had a hard childhood, which led to a drinking problem, which led to money and relationship problems, which led to the streets, we theorised. We could only imagine the horrible misfortunes that these poor men, and occasionally women, suffered.

Campbell & Graham partnered with various homeless charities, organising events, sleep-outs, raffles, and suchlike to fundraise. We all took part and did what we could to make ourselves feel better about the whole thing. We donated clothes to shelters and gave monetary donations at Christmas to Black Santa, the priest who collected donations outside St Anne's Cathedral every December. All our charitable activities were photographed, showcased on our websites, and included in our work pitches, of course. *Look how much we care!*

Despite how often we quoted the old tropes of 'It could happen to anyone!' or 'We're all only three pay cheques away from the streets ourselves!' there was a sense of surety that this only happened to other people; not to people like us.

So, I can't tell you how much it shocked me, and I mean *really* shocked me, when I made eye contact with one of the homeless guys one morning and realised that the man before me, wrapped in a filthy, tatty sleeping bag, holding a coffee cup with 'change please' written on it, was in my year at school!

It just couldn't be possible. We went to a Grammar School for Christ's sake! We locked eyes, and it felt like I passed him in slow motion. He had retained some of his handsomeness, even with the dirty beard and greasy long hair. He was thinner than he'd been in school, but it gave him an angular, heroin-chic look. His eyes were piercing blue and clear, unlike many of his contemporaries.

When I tried to speak to him, I stuttered, "P-P-Paul, gosh is that you? What have you been up to?" I cringe when I think of it now. Asking what he'd been up to. Aghh! He noted my embarrassment and didn't answer. Instead, he said, "Look at you! Hot shot... something or other? Banker?" I laughed like he'd just told a great joke, "Close, solicitor!"

We chatted awkwardly, me pointedly not asking why he was on the streets or if he needed help, while leaning over him, as he remained sitting on the pavement with a calm smile. As we spoke, I started to feel uneasy. Now, looking back, I can try to dismiss it as fear of being asked for money, or if he could stay at my house for a few days, or, more likely, fear that my own risk of becoming homeless wasn't as far-fetched as I liked to think. Christ, I owed over £40k in student loans and £10k on credit cards. But no. When I think back on it, the fear I felt was something else. There was something unnerving about him.

Conscious of time, I laughed nervously. "Right! Best be off. These cases won't win themselves, ha-ha!" He stopped smiling then and leaned back a bit. We kept eye contact as I straightened.

"Well," I said, pointlessly. Words stuck in my throat. "Em, Paul, do you..."

"A tenner'd be great. *If* you can spare it."

His sarcasm made me blush, and I was all fingers and thumbs with a suddenly impenetrable purse. I fished out my only note, a twenty. Would giving that make me look even more patronising? Well, I couldn't *not* give it. I handed the twenty pound note out for him to take. Moments passed as he held my gaze with those pitiless blue eyes. It was like locking eyes with a wolf. Tension built as I stood awkwardly with the note in his face. Was he going to refuse to take it?

Suddenly, his arm shot out, and he gripped my hand, squeezing it so tightly that I cried out in pain. People turned to look at us, but I resisted the urge to call out for help and kept eye contact with Paul.

I kept my voice steady, even as my heart thumped in my chest. “Paul. It’s been good to see you, but I have to go now,” I said before yanking my throbbing hand back, leaving the crumpled note in Paul’s grasp. I felt a scratch on my palm. Paul kept his dead gaze on me as I turned and hurried away.

Turning the corner onto another street, I stole a glance back at Paul, and could swear he was licking his hand. Licking off the blood he’d just drawn from me. Shuddering, I practically ran to my office.

When I got to the office, I must have looked awful. The scratch on my palm was still bleeding, and there was blood on my woollen coat. My co-workers flocked over, “Jeez LA, what happened to you? Are you okay?”

“Yeah, fine,” I said. Because we always say that, don’t we? Then I told them what happened but I implied that I was upset because I saw an old school friend sleeping on the street, then tripped and fell on the walk back to the office. I couldn’t find the words to say I was frightened of a homeless man. We were their champions! “What an awful morning!” The co-workers empathised, fetching me the first aid kit. I used three alcohol wipes on the cut, mindful of Paul’s filthy fingernails.

One of my team, Anne, was the year above me in school. We’d become good friends in work and I told her more of the story over lunch when it was just the two of us.

"Paul Cartwright? No way!" She gushed excitedly. "Do you remember how *everyone* thought he was such a ride? When I think of how he could have had his pick of girls and the perfect life."

"Didn't he date that girl in the year below you? Can't think of her name now. The girls in my year were right bitches to her. Just jealous. Although for someone who was dating the hottest boy in school, she always looked bloody miserable."

Anne was right, I remembered Paul dating someone and it had surprised everyone. I couldn't remember her name, but I could picture her. Not quite ugly but not beautiful. Not sporty and not overly popular. She just...made up the numbers. Likely a civil servant now. Anne was a total cow in school and quite likely led any bitchy campaigns. She'd mellowed a bit in her twenties, thankfully.

"And come here," Anne continued, hitting her stride as the memories came back, "wasn't there some scandal about a fight in the boys changing room? Poor Ricky whatsiface with the fractured skull? Some boys said they were messing round and Ricky slipped. Others said, no – Paul smacked his head off the tiles a few times over some stupid comment Ricky made."

"Oh yeah. I'd forgotten about the changing room incident. The school hushed it all up, didn't they? I think that guy Ricky had to re-sit his A Levels at Tech the following year."

"Yeah, he was off school for ages recovering, poor fella." Anne continued.

Anne's comment made me think of Paul's unnerving gaze and the scratch on my hand. He'd hurt me deliberately while I was trying to help him. From that day on, I varied my route to work, so I never again went down that same street where I'd seen Paul. I started checking every street for signs of Paul before walking down them, scanning the face of every homeless person to the point where I was probably making *them* nervous. Then, eventually, as the weeks and months passed, I started to think less about him.

I honestly think if I hadn't run into his bloody ex-girlfriend, that would have been the end of it. But no. Months later, while I was out for Christmas drinks at a Chinese restaurant slash karaoke bar, I looked up to see Paul outside the restaurant looking in. I jumped, startled to see him. He didn't look homeless; he looked well-dressed and presentable. He didn't notice me as he was staring across the restaurant, to my right. I glanced over and started. His old girlfriend from school was with a group of clearly well-oiled mates. In the moment between me looking at her and looking back to the street, Paul was gone. I wondered if he was following her.

Intrigued and slightly worried, I kept half an eye on her as I ordered and had dinner with my friends. When we'd finished and were heading to the bar section of the venue for the karaoke, I saw her heading for the toilets and followed her. I was one behind her in the inevitable queue. When she spotted me, I gave an awkward half-wave. As recognition dawned on her, she turned to me with a wide smile. "Hi LA, it's great to see you!"

"You too!" I begged my subconscious for a name. "What are you up to these days?"

Our brief chat continued as the queue diminished. We broke apart to go into the disgusting cubicles, and I tried bribing my subconscious with more white wine if it would tell me her bloody name. Nothing doing. We met again at the sinks.

"It's Gemma, by the way," she said with a knowing smirk.

"Sorry, yes! Gemma. Ah! I've always been shit at remembering names. It's nice to see you again, Gemma." We smiled tipsily at each other and, as we made our way back to the increasingly noisy bar, without really thinking, I blurted out, "Hey, guess who I saw a few weeks ago, Paul Cartwright! Did you guys keep in touch?" The change in her demeanour was instant. She looked furious. "Keep in touch? With Paul? Are you fucking joking?"

She scowled and scanned the room for her friends. "Fuck sakes," she muttered. Her mates were next up for a karaoke song and were gesturing for her to hurry up. 'I Touch Myself' by the Divinyls was on the screen. "No way!" she shouted over to them, waving her arms. I didn't blame her and I saw an opportunity.

"Can I buy you a drink?"

"Oh, I don't know," she said, arms wrapped around herself.

"Please. My way of saying sorry for forgetting your name. One drink!"

Gemma reluctantly agreed and we headed to the bar. I ordered large wines for us both and gestured to a marginally quieter area at the back of the bar.

"Sorry Gemma, I didn't mean to hit a nerve by mentioning Paul."

She rolled her eyes and looked away, gulping her wine.

"I only brought him up because when I saw him a few months ago, he was on the streets. I was just so shocked. I never knew anyone who ended up homeless before."

She turned to face me, eyes narrow. "*When* did you see him?"

I decided not to mention that I'd seen him earlier that evening, in case I freaked her out. "Um, it was a few months ago now."

"When exactly, LA?"

Did she know I was lying? "Err, I want to say August?"

"Did you hear that he died?" Gemma asked.

"What?! No, he didn't. Why would you say that?"

"Oh, he died alright. End of September. It came up on my Facebook feed. His sister was connected to friends of mine who commented on her posts."

I was gobsmacked. Paul wasn't dead, I just saw him! I looked over to the window again, but of course, there was no sign. Had I seen him? It was only a glimpse. And he had looked good, not at all like the last time I saw him. I must have been mistaken.

Gemma was still looking at me closely. "*Where* did you see him?" She asked.

"Castle Lane, near Cornmarket. He was with a few other homeless men."

"Hmm, maybe with his murderer. He didn't die of an overdose like you might think. Someone bashed his brains in."

"Shit."

"Yeah. Shit indeed, LA."

Confused, I couldn't think of anything else to say. I didn't want to accuse her of lying. If Facebook was the sole source of her information, it was possible she was mistaken. As we stood in silence, I realised her friends were no longer on stage. Gemma turned with a wry smile, clearly about to make her excuses.

"Did things not end well with you and Paul?"

She raised her eyebrows sardonically, "What makes you say that?"

"Well, for starters, you don't seem remotely sad that he was murdered on the streets."

"No. Things didn't end well," she sighed. "Fuck it, I need a fag. Get me another Pinot Grigio and meet me outside. I'll tell my mates I'll be with them in a minute."

I rushed to the bar, desperate to get served before she changed her mind again. Wines in hand, I scooted outside to meet her, hoping the smokers' area had an outside heater. It didn't. Gemma puffed on a Marlborough Light as I poured our mini wine bottles into our glasses.

"So, yeah. I was as surprised as anyone that Paul wanted to date me. I wasn't pretty or popular."

She waved her hands to shoo away my efforts to protest. "Yeah, yeah, yeah, we're all beautiful on the inside. You can tell me how pretty I am later. Just let me tell my story." She pulled on her cigarette, suddenly looking tired and older than her years.

"Where was I? Oh yeah, so Paul started walking me home from school and ringing me in the evenings. He left little notes in my locker and gave me long looks in the corridor. I was flattered; who wouldn't be? He was Paul fucking Cartwright. He was the best-looking boy in Lower Sixth, and I was a Fifth Year nobody. I was suspicious, though; I do remember that. And I was wary of attracting unwanted attention. Those bitches in Upper Sixth got wind of him liking me and they were hard to avoid. But his flattery worked."

"We started meeting up in town, going to the cinema or bowling, you know, the usual. Then we started going to his house. I hadn't dated before. God! It's so embarrassing now but it took me a while to realise that things were really, really off. For one thing, he didn't drink. Do you remember how desperate we all were to be pissed all the time? Paul said he didn't like feeling out of control, but he'd always buy me drinks with his fake ID. I didn't like drinking and was terrified of being caught drunk by my parents, as I was only sixteen. "

"But when Paul bought me drink, I *had* to drink it. Half bottles of vodka, practically neat. He'd stand over me, feeding me sips and telling me how cute I looked when I was pissed. I didn't feel cute, I felt sick and out of control."

Gemma threw back her wine, gulping down most of the glass in one go, flinching as she swallowed it.

"Then, he'd undress me but not touch me. Just get me pissed, remove my top and bra and make me sit there in front of him, giving me orders not to move, stand or look at him. It could last for hours. I was mortified, but too cowed to refuse."

"Other times, he'd make me face his bedroom door, telling me not to turn around. He'd lift my school skirt, tuck it into the waistband and remove my knickers. Then he'd listen to music, do homework or work out. For hours! While I just stood facing the door, not allowed to look round; tipsy from the vodka or whatever he'd made me drink at 4pm and dying of embarrassment cause my arse was out."

"It sounds so stupid now, and God, I have questioned myself since then. I was scared of him.

He was a lot bigger and stronger than I was, yes, but that doesn't fully explain it. He didn't hit me or even threaten to, but he still *really* scared me. He'd stare at me with those blue eyes and my stomach would be in knots."

"After a couple of months, things kicked up a notch. He'd lie me on the bed and straddle me, sitting on my belly, pinning my hands under his knees and... just stare at me. I'd end up in tears and eventually beg him to get off me. I'd even apologise, hoping he'd stop punishing me if I said sorry. He never listened. Eventually, I realised why his staring at me scared me so much. He looked like he was trying to make a decision, but I had no idea what options he was weighing up."

Gemma dragged on the remains of her cigarette again before stubbing it out under her toe. I had forgotten the cold. I remembered Paul's stare while he grasped my hand and the fear I'd felt in those brief moments. Poor Gemma must have been terrified. She swigged the dregs of her wine before continuing.

"He never kissed me. Not once. Everyone was so jealous of us dating, and my Mum kept trying to have chats about being careful and using protection. But there was no kissing, no hand holding. He didn't fancy me. Hell, he didn't even like me!"

"So, that begged the question, what did he want with me? Why were we spending all this time together?"

"His family was a weird bunch. His Mum and Dad spoke to him, his sister and me as if we were all acquaintances who bumped into each other in a golf club. They wouldn't offer me a cup of tea, let alone ask me to stay for dinner. If I was there over dinner time, I'd sit in Paul's room waiting for them to finish."

"His younger sister, Lizzy, was the nicest of the lot. You probably didn't know her. She was a few years younger than he was, and she went to the same posh girls' school her Mum had gone to. She always seemed a bit lost in that house, as if she was a foreign exchange student everyone politely tolerated. I think she wanted us to talk more than we did but Paul always kept me in his room, away from everyone."

"When he'd release me, I'd just quietly let myself out. It was a fifty-minute walk home. They had three cars in the driveway and not one of them would offer me a lift home in the dark. Not that I would have taken a lift from his parents; they might have smelled the drink. The walk gave me a chance to sober up. Of course, I should have stopped meeting him, or I could have told my parents I didn't want to see him anymore. They would have helped me end it. I could have helped myself in a thousand ways. I honestly can't explain why I didn't."

I was about to say something reassuring when we were interrupted by one of Gemma's friends coming out to look for her.

"Yaarrite love?" she slurred when she spotted us. "We're headed to Angie's guy's thingy now. Ya comin'?"

"Yes. Grab my coat and meet me back here with Angie." Gemma handed me her wine glass and rubbed her arms for warmth.

"And then things escalated," she said without emotion. We locked eyes for a second before she welled up and looked away. Voice cracking, she continued.

"When we were alone in his house, after school before his parents came home, he continued to sit on top of me; only he moved up to sit on my chest, still pinning my arms by my side under his legs. He was too heavy. It hurt my breasts and I struggled to breathe. He'd play music to mask any noises I made."

"Then..." she took a deep breath before continuing, "then he'd tilt my head back and force his fingers into my mouth. All his fingers, deep in my throat, wiggling them at the back to make me gag. I'd buck and thrash beneath him, but he wouldn't stop. I'd retch and vomit, and he would stop to let me spit the vomit onto the towel he had already placed on the pillow to catch it. The same sequence would be repeated. Open mouth, push in fingers. Wiggle fingers to make me gag. Watch me retch and vomit in my mouth. Remove fingers to let me spit up and gasp to catch my breath. Then repeat. Over and over. And all the while, Paul would be cool as a cucumber, not even sweating; just watching me like he was conducting a science experiment. This went on for about a month. By the end, it would last for thirty minutes at a time."

"Jesus Gemma, he could have killed you!" I said, stunned.

Gemma raised an eyebrow and smiled wryly at me. "I truly believe he was building up to it. He was either still trying to summon up the courage to do it, or he didn't want to do it too soon because he'd have to find someone to replace me. It was pretty clever. If I died, he'd claim I choked in my sleep while he was downstairs. He'd say that I had a drinking problem. There'd be no signs of struggle and there would be alcohol in my system.

Meanwhile, my life was unravelling. I woke up with dread in my stomach every day. I lost weight. I looked awful, pale and drawn with dark bags under my eyes. I couldn't concentrate in class or at home and started skipping school to avoid Paul. Teachers were calling my parents who finally seemed to cop on that things weren't great. I think Paul started worrying that I'd tell someone what was happening. I was leaving school one day when he pulled up beside me in his car. There were a lot of kids around. He asked me to get in. I didn't want to and hesitated on the pavement. He turned on the charm and said "Please Gemma, come on. Let me apologise."

"People were starting to stare and, for reasons I'll never truly understand, I got in. Paul's mask of kindness fell the second we sped off. We drove in silence to his home, and my panic was rising. He opened the car door for me and steered me into the house by the arm. As we climbed the stairs to his room, a real sense of terror started to overcome me but it was like I was watching myself from three paces back, screaming at myself from afar. As we passed his sister's room on the landing, she and I locked eyes. She got off her bed and padded to her bedroom door, watching Paul and me as we entered his room, before he shut his door behind us."

"Paul put on loud music and told me to lie down on the bed. At that moment, I reacted and tried to get to the door. He easily overpowered me and pushed me onto the bed, climbing on top of me. He clamped his hand over my mouth and took a few moments to calm himself before reaching for the towel. Then he stopped himself. No need for a towel or alcohol this time. He looked excited. Terror filled my whole body. Paul grasped the back of my hair in his hand, pulled my head back and calmly began pushing his hand into my mouth. This was it, what he had been building up to for months. When the gagging started, I prayed for help. I thought about my family. What cause of death would they be told? Accidental choking? Murder? Manslaughter? Would they spend years wondering why I hadn't asked for help? Or would they believe Paul and comfort him at my funeral? I retched. Vomit filled my throat as Paul's hand dug deeper, sealing it in. I couldn't breathe. I bucked and kicked but Paul was relentless. He looked completely calm. I remember hoping that dying wouldn't take too long. I squeezed my eyes shut."

Click!

"My eyes flew open. Paul and I turned to see Lizzy at the door, taking a picture of us with an old camera. For a split second, everyone froze."

"Lizzy lowered the camera and made eye contact with Paul, defiant and unapologetic."

"Then, she bolted."

"Paul swore, leapt off me and started after her. He was big and athletic, Lizzy was skinny and quick. She raced down the stairs, Paul thundering behind her. I leaned over to vomit on the floor, then lay panting for a second, catching my breath, listening to them tear noisily through the house. Then, finally, *finally* it was like my head and body collided back together."

Move!

"I rolled off the bed and stumbled downstairs on shaking legs. Paul and Lizzy had gone out to the back garden. I could hear him shouting angrily at her. I grabbed my bag from the hall, rushed out the front door, and ran home. As I ran, I fished my phone out of my bag and called my Dad, checking over my shoulder very few steps. I could hardly speak but mumbled enough about breaking up with Paul for him to come and get me. Dad begged me to tell the truth as I was so shaken up, but I just couldn't bring myself to. Later, I told him and Mum some half-truths and some outright lies. They didn't believe me, but I refused to say anymore. Instead, I begged them to let me change schools, blaming it on the bullying from the older girls and the break-up with Paul. They weren't happy about it at first, but they let me do it. I was immediately accepted to an under-subscribed secondary school which turned out to be fantastic."

"So, I didn't see Paul again after that. I never saw Lizzy again either, so I never got the chance to thank her. She saved my life; I've no doubt of that. I heard Paul moved to Edinburgh to go to Uni there."

"Friends from school who went to Glasgow and Edinburgh kept me updated on him, assuming I'd be interested."

"First, they told me he was expelled for plagiarism, then he had a short spell in prison for assault. It was quite the scandal. They didn't know when he developed his addiction problem but, after jail, they heard he ended up homeless. His friends were always surprised that his family didn't help him more. They hadn't met his family. Rumour had it that he had to move back to Northern Ireland as he was threatened in Edinburgh. And that," said Gemma, pulling on her coat, "is all I have to tell you."

Fellow smokers had stopped pretending to eavesdrop and were openly gawking as she told her story. Gemma's friends were flanking her now, eager to be off. One gave me a sour look, clearly unhappy that I'd pressed Gemma to tell such an unhappy tale. I apologised to Gemma and hugged her before she left, before heading inside to warm up and find my friends.

Weeks passed, and I couldn't get Gemma's story out of my head. It was like when you see a disturbing scene in a movie, a fingernail being torn off or a limb snapped with bone jutting out. The image of Gemma with Paul on top of her, unable to move with fingers forced down her throat, kept replaying in my mind, making me twitchy. I found myself retching and gagging for no reason. I would paw anxiously at my own throat.

Then, when I was rushing through town one rainy morning, a man standing outside a shop swivelled his head toward me, then away again, and I could have sworn it was Paul. I stopped dead, heart pounding. Surely Gemma was wrong? I hadn't checked for Paul's obituary online; I'd just taken her at her word. I walked towards the man until I could see his reflection in the window. It wasn't Paul; just stress, lack of coffee, tiredness, or all three.

Less than a week later, I saw him again. I was holding a blazer up against me in front of a mirror in M&S, when I spotted him behind me, glaring at my reflection. There was no mistaking those blue eyes. I whipped my head around, but he was gone in the blink of an eye. I left without buying the blazer and made an excuse to take the afternoon off work.

I googled him that afternoon, wondering why I'd left it so long. Gemma was right, he was buried at the end of September. It was mid-January now. Online searches revealed an uncomfortable medley of touching posts from relatives with cute childhood photos, and quite a few court appearances and convictions for Paul, including photos of him looking haggard and shifty.

I *must* have been mistaken when I spotted him. Every time I spotted him. I kept telling myself that, but my nerves started to unravel and I found myself searching for his face everywhere I went. I started to avoid crowds. I didn't want to go to court and made excuses to stay at my desk. I stopped seeing friends and had groceries delivered. I only left the house for my commute to and from the office or to go to my Mum's house. It worked; I saw nothing for months. I became hopeful.

Then, suddenly, he appeared closer to home. I lived in Dundonald back then if you remember? In a semi-detached shoe box. I lost years of my life getting the bus in and out of Belfast city centre every day. On the bus home one evening, I was looking out the window when we passed a chip shop near the Ulster Hospital. A man was standing outside. He looked up as the bus passed and we locked eyes. It was Paul. No mistake. I retched and burst into tears. Panic set in and I could hardly get a breath. But it was followed by rage. This couldn't go on.

I jumped off at the next stop and marched back to the chip shop as fast as I could. I grabbed the man's arm and spun him roughly around to face me, ready for a fight. Of course, it wasn't him. It looked fuck all like him. Not even the right age range.

I'd scared the life out of some poor bloke, who was understandably furious at being ambushed by a madwoman. I made a right show of myself, offering grovelling apologies in front of the whole chippie queue before trudging home, cheeks burning and feet killing me.

I spent that night the same way I had been spending every night; searching and re-reading the Obits and Facebook posts about Paul's death. I willed the written evidence of his death to blow away the spectre of him, even as my paranoia conspired against me. What if someone else was beaten to a pulp and it was wrongly assumed to be Paul? The worry of whether or not I was crazy was relentless. It wasn't much of a stretch to consider that reading Paul's online tributes and looking at his obituary photo on a nightly basis was causing me to see him during the day. I hated that I couldn't trust myself.

I hardly slept again that night, but by then I was on a written warning for absence and had run out of enhanced sick pay. I wasn't well enough to go in to work, and I couldn't afford to be off. So, I did what was becoming standard for me; I turned up at the office and did a shit job, while struggling to stay awake at my desk.

My workmates weren't even annoyed by my shitty efforts by then. Instead they pitied me, which was worse. My line manager had already asked if I'd consider seeing someone. I told her seeing someone was the problem and had laughed too loudly at my own joke. She stopped meeting me on her own after that. My career and sanity were hanging by a thread. I couldn't imagine how things could get any worse.

How wrong I was.

My little shoe box home was just that, mine. I bought it without any help and had paid for everything in it, every bill. Even when the insomnia hit, it was never because I felt afraid in my own house. It was my sanctuary. I arrived home on the night in question jittery and teary. I flung my coat, bag and brolly in a heap in the hall, went into my kitchen and plonked myself at the dining table. I was contemplating when, not *if*, I should open wine, when my eyes were drawn to the middle of the dining table. On it sat a crumpled, blood-stained twenty pound note.

My thoughts froze and my stomach lurched. I stopped breathing.

I thought I had panicked before, but I was wrong. It was nothing like how I felt now. I looked anxiously around the room and, when I stood up, everything spun around me. My heart was beating so hard that I thought I might pass out. Blood whooshed through my ears. I couldn't draw breath. I stared at the bloodied note. That table was clear when I left that morning. No one had been in my house.

I know what you're thinking. I've gone over this story so many times with counsellors, friends and family, who all think they *know* that I had forgotten I'd left the money on the table myself. There's no other explanation. I was tired and overwrought. But *I know.*

I *know* I cleared my dishes off my dining table that morning, wiped it down and left it bare. I *know* I stopped to get money out of the ATM on my walk to the bus stop that morning because I needed cash. I *know* I did NOT leave a blood-stained, crumpled twenty-pound note in the middle of my dining table.

Someone had been, or was still, in my house!

I went out the back door and stood in the cool air until the worst of the panic subsided and I could gather myself. I left the back door open, walked cautiously down the hall, and opened the front door, my rationale being that either the intruder or I could run out easily if we found each other. Then, and I still don't know how I mustered the courage for this, I slowly and methodically checked every room. I found no one and no trace of anyone having been in any other room. I came back downstairs, closed the doors, went back to the table, and sat staring at the note.

Of course, I considered calling the police. But to say what? To report a burglar who broke in and left dirty money on my dining table? What if I lost the run of myself altogether and told them I was being haunted by a dead homeless guy from school, who'd tried to vomit a girl to death?

I wanted to call my Mum but she was worried enough about me already. So, I called no one. I stayed at the table, staring at the note until it became dark, and I went upstairs, got ready for bed and checked the bedrooms again. Empty.

I climbed into bed, even though I knew there was no chance of sleep. But sure, what else do you do at night? I turned off the lights, lay back and closed my eyes. Then...

Click!!

The unmistakable sound of an old camera, just by my ear.

Two things happened at once. I started to raise my head off my pillow, and two large arms lifted from either side of my pillow, clamped onto my face, and pulled me back down.

Blind terror consumed me. The hands squeezed my face, covered my eyes and pinched my nose. When I opened my mouth to scream, cold, fetid fingers pushed in. I retched. I fought. I clawed at the hands. I writhed and bucked. It was no use. The hands held my head tight, and the fingers wormed deeper into my mouth. Bile filled my throat. I tried to fight the panic. I reached out, feeling for anything to help. My phone was beside me and my bed was under the window. I swung my arm and flung the phone hard at the window. It bounced off, back onto the bottom of the bed.

"Did you hear that?" "Hear what?" My neighbours' voices drifted up from outside.

The fingers on one hand pressed harder into my eye socket. The fingers on the other dug further into my throat. I retched again and pulled on the arm with one hand while I reached to find my phone with my other. I could just feel the phone with my fingertips. I stretched but couldn't reach it. Then I needed both hands to tug on the arms again.

I felt my eye popping. It was strangely painless. I retched again, and vomit exploded in my throat, trapped. In desperation, I felt for my phone with my foot. Once located, I pressed it under my heel and tried to drag it up the bed. My fingers scrabbled towards it until I could just grasp it. I curled it into my hand, mustered my strength and hurled it as hard as I could at the window.

Bang!

"LA? Is that you? Yaarite love?"

"What do you think's going on?"

"How would I know?"

A knock at the door.

I thumped the mattress with my feet.

"Should we go in?"

"Does she still keep a key under the plant pot?"

I gagged and choked. I felt eye goo run down my temples. I was sure this was the end.

My front door opened.

"LA?! You there?"

I kicked my legs hard on the mattress again, trying desperately to be heard. The hands dug in harder, urgently.

I thumped and clawed at them. It was no use.

I couldn't breathe. I was dying.

Then, two more things happened at once. My bedroom door flung open and the couple from next door rushed in, and the hands vanished.

My neighbours, Neil and Laura, raced to me and turned me over. Vomit fell out onto the carpet, but my throat was still blocked. I couldn't draw breath. My sight was dark.

Neil pulled me off the bed and onto my knees, leaning me over the mattress. He put his arms around me and started the Heimlich manoeuvre.

"One. Two, Three, Heave!"

It didn't work, and it hurt like hell. My arms flailed.

"DO SOMETHING!" his wife, Laura, screamed at him.

"I AM TRYING!" he screamed back. "One, two three, HEAVE!"

Neil tried the Heimlich again. It didn't work. I felt a sharp pain in my ribs. I wanted to shout at him to stop. That it was too late. I was resigned to dying. I just wanted them to leave me alone.

"NEEEILLL! FUCKING HELP HER!"

"WHAT DO YOU THINK I'M DOING!!! Ring the fuckin' ambulance would ye!"

He lifted me up a bit.

"COME ON LA!" he screamed. "ONE! TWO! THREE! HURRGH!"

Neil roared as he rammed hard under my stomach until, finally, vomit shot out, and I was able desperately to gulp in some air. Relief flooded me as I coughed and cried. Jesus, it hurt. I fell to the floor, clutching my side and my eye. Laura was on her knees, sobbing with relief while trying to speak to the emergency operator.

Neil cried too, saying "Oh God. Oh God," over and over again.

The ambulance arrived soon after. I spent over a week in The Ulster Hospital getting my eye and ribs seen to. They tried their best, but my eye was ruined.

Then, naturally, they sectioned me. They said I'd had Sleep Deprivation Psychosis. I spent almost four weeks under observation. To leave, I had to accept and repeat their version of events...

'Extreme exhaustion caused hallucinations and insomnia before causing a seizure. The seizure made me vomit and I'd choked on it. I clawed and bruised my own face when I was choking. I stuck my finger in my eye and damaged it myself. There were no arms under my pillow. I hadn't been seeing a dead homeless guy all over Belfast for months. It. Was. All. In. My. Head.'

I sold the house. In fact, I never entered it again. I resigned from my job and didn't work for almost a year. Mum was fantastic. She sorted everything. She hadn't been expecting her hotshot lawyer daughter to boomerang back home and start sleeping with the light on. But she never complained, and she never said she didn't believe me. It was nice being back at home, just us two. I saw a counsellor once a week and, slowly, I got better. Eventually, I took a job as a legal advisor for a charity and enjoyed it more than I thought I would, even though the pay was shit. When I was ready, I moved out into a rental flat and life went on. I got better jobs. I got better with people. And I never saw Paul again.

Hardly anyone believes me, and I don't blame them. But I know it was real. It happened. I was almost killed in my bed, and it wasn't because of a fucking seizure."

Chapter 3

The Gathering, 19:15

Good grief! Is this what passes for entertainment in leafy South Belfast? Telling a room full of people about your stress-induced mental breakdown repackaged and gussied up as a ghost story?

I'm still looking at LA when she pokes out her glass eye, pops it in her mouth for a few seconds, then spits it out and pops it back into its socket. I stare at her, unable to look away. Ameera gives me a sharp nudge in the ribs and I snap my mouth shut. An awkwardness falls. Wine glasses are refilled. People nibble. LA looks pale but defiant.

"Well, I for one believe you." says Eleanor in a patronising tone, patting LA's hand. *Liar*, I think. A general murmur of agreement goes round the table, but I spy Sarah and Ameera making eyes at each other. Interesting. I'm not the only sceptic. Why are they here then?

"Did they ever get anyone for Paul's murder, LA?" asks Lydia, bossily, like it was LA's fault somehow if they hadn't.

"No. No one was ever charged. I think the case is technically still open, but I doubt they're looking too hard," LA answers.

We continue to look at each other awkwardly until Joanna jumps up to check on the food. "Time for one more story if we want the Bombay Potatoes really crispy!" She shouts, slamming the Aga door shut. "Honestly, do not believe the hype about bloody Agas! You open the top to heat the chilli, and the oven temperature drops like a stone. I don't get what all the fuss is about."

Next time I want to save ten grand, I'll be sure to remember that. Thanks, Joanna! The group look at each other expectantly while I look at the table, twisting my napkin in my hands.

Mercifully, Sarah is next to tell her story.

Chapter 4

Sarah's Story – 'The Girl in the Waiting Room'

~~~

Sarah: *Bloody Joanna! I've been dreading tonight. She is so friggin' pushy. Forever coming up with plans that always sound so reasonable when you're with her. It's only when you reflect on the conversation afterwards that you realise what she's really asking.*

LA was right; it would be so much nicer to be out in a nice restaurant in town, catching up on everyone's craic instead of this organised fun.

But I've committed to it now so I must see it through.

And if I'm being honest, retelling the tales really does help. It's too easy to look back on your experiences and start gaslighting yourself into thinking 'maybe it didn't really happen.' 'I was overworked.' 'There must have been a rational explanation.' But no. There was no explanation for what happened to me.

Ghost stories are funny things. About half the people you talk to have one of their own, and swear blind it's true. The other half have never seen a thing, and are left to decide whether the storytellers are
~~~

recounting events as they saw it, but are mistaken, deluded, mad, hallucinating, sleep-deprived, poisoned by carbon monoxide, off their tits on drugs, or, some winning combination of all of the aforementioned.

Or maybe, of course, they're just making it up for the craic.

I had this very dilemma with a patient years ago who came into surgery a nervous wreck, convinced she had a brain tumour. She lived in a new-build apartment, and every time she looked in her bathroom mirror, she swore she saw a dead-eyed child sitting in the bath, staring back at her. Blue with cold. Wasted with neglect.

Naturally, I tested her for drugs first. Negative. No tumours either. Given my own experiences, I advised her to move. She did and in doing so, switched GP. So I never found out if that solved the problem.

Experiences of the unexplained are a bit like illnesses that way. You could be a forty-a-day smoker for decades and be cancer free. Or be a twenty year old gym bunny who is ravaged by it.

Take Ada, Joanna's sister. That poor woman had bad luck every which way she turned. It wasn't right.

I'd do anything to help her.

Anything.

But first, I have to get through this bloody evening. I'll rely on my usual supports. Throwing back the wine like it's my last night on earth. Eating all Joanna's good food and telling the most outrageous stories from work, not letting the truth get in the way of a good laugh.

I can do this. Let's go.

~~~

"My encounter happened when I had just qualified as a doctor, also back in the noughties, a few years after LA's experience with Paul. As most of you know, Ameera and I were at Queen's University Medical School together. When we graduated, we both joined GP surgeries to start our Foundation Year, the first step on the road to becoming GPs or Consultants. We could finally earn some money and pay back our student loans.

To say that all GP surgeries in Northern Ireland are not the same is quite the understatement. Ameera got one in fucking Holywood, where she spent her days convincing Range Rover driving Mums that their chubby cherubs had constipation, not appendicitis. I still don't know who you blew for that cushy placement, Ameera!
~~~

I, on the other hand, had to take a shitty temporary post at a surgery beside a rough-as-fuck estate in North Belfast. There were always vacancies there because almost all the other GPs were off on stress-related sick leave. Practically the whole surgery was run by medical students or recently qualified docs. There was only one experienced doctor there, Dr Johnston, who worked two mornings a week! He spent those mornings either gossiping with the patients about the state of the country or moaning with the receptionists about how lazy the next generation of doctors were. He was supposed to give the rest of us advice and guidance. Ha! That was a laugh! If we ever asked a question about a patient with complex needs, he would take off his glasses, peer down his nose at us and sneer, "Oh my goodness. My, my, my. Did they not teach you that in the entire five years you were at Queen's? Hmm? Why, I've a mind to ring the Medical School myself and demand to know why they've left something so important off the curriculum. What do you think they'll say? Hmm?" Then he'd put his glasses back on and wave us away. Self-important, pompous wanker! We were on our own.

There were three other Foundation Year or post-graduate doctors with me plus students on placement rotations. The workload was enormous. We had planned appointments from 10am to 4pm.

Emergency walk-ins were permitted from 8:30am to 10am and after 4pm. We could have had 30 people turn up in the morning and only get through half of them. Then the rest would just stay! In theory, they should have come back after 4pm when the next emergency slots were open, but they knew the receptionists would squeeze them in if we had any no-shows. And besides, the surgery was like a fucking social hub. People brought newspapers, sandwiches and flasks of tea. They hung around moaning and gossiping, napping and reading in the chairs. It was like Paddy's Market.

In fairness to the Pitbulls on reception, they took no shit. It didn't matter what was wrong with the patients, if they were bleeding over the carpet, or who their Da was, they all had to wait their turn. They took no shit from us either. We didn't get so much as a cup of tea without their permission, but they did make sure we got a thirty-minute lunch every day. And, oh my goodness, we needed it. Being in that wee office with patients arriving every ten minutes was like being under siege. Some of them wanted to be diagnosed with random shit they knew would get them more benefits, like schizofuckingphrenia. Oh aye, 'cause it'll take a local GP ten minutes to diagnose that! The few who actually worked all wanted sick notes. The druggies wanted drugs, as did the hypochondriacs. And the patients that actually were sick, you couldn't help anyway! Waiting lists were atrocious, even then. People needing knee replacements, hip replacements, hearing aids, heart surgery, cancer diagnoses or MRIs all kept turning up to beg for more pain relief and demand to know why they hadn't seen a consultant yet.

We had to break it to them that, while they'd been told they had a three-year wait a year ago, it was now a four-year wait. "Yes, I am aware the maths doesn't make sense. There's no need to scream at me, madam! Here's a tissue. Please stop crying. Perhaps you could try talking to your local politician?"

It was so demoralising. We didn't even raise the option of them going private. No point. No one had any money round there. Well, the drug dealers did, but they'd sooner buy a Porsche than buy their Ma a new hip. The surgery should have closed to patients at 5pm. The Pitbulls left on time every evening, but the patients stayed. It was hard to turn them away, and we knew they'd just be back the next morning, making the next day's queue even longer. Some of them even point-blank refused to leave until we saw them. What could we do? Manhandle them out the door? You didn't see these guys. Ring the police? They were busier than us round there! And trust me, you didn't mess with these locals lightly.

So, we'd man the reception desk ourselves and try to get them all seen and out the door as swiftly as possible. If we got locked up and away before 7.30pm, we were doing well. The friendship and support from the other doctors were the only things that made it bearable. We'd all known each other in Queens to varying degrees, having crossed paths during lectures or clinical placements. Some of us had rowed together in the Queen's Rowing Club, dated friends or each other and hung out at the same parties and clubs.

One of the doctors, Freddie, had been a couple of years above me in Uni and was a rower like me. We had gone to a lot of the same regattas all over Ireland and GB. We hit it off and had sort of dated. Well, we'd shagged a lot. He was gorgeous and great craic. Not one for settling down though; he was a right dog. I think he was one of the first in his family to go to university. I wasn't sure exactly where he was from in Belfast, but he was never as shocked by some of the stories as the rest of us. His Dad had been injured by a car bomb that killed his aunt, I knew that much. He'd more patience than the rest of us and took on the work Dr Johnston should have been doing, helping with tricky cases and keeping morale up. And we still shagged. A lot. I'd like to blame it on the war mentality; as I said, working there felt like being under siege. But hey, maybe we were just young, single and horny. We would send the others on home by offering to lock up once the last of the walking wounded finally shuffled off, then go at it in one of our surgeries.

I'd like to say I feel ashamed of myself when I look back. I mean, it wasn't exactly professional. But it was so much *fun*. I would be a patient, and Freddie would be my doctor. "What can I help with today, Miss?" He'd say lifting me onto his examination bed. "Every time my husband is away with work, I get this tingling between my legs, and I can't make it stop. It's very distracting." "Can you show me where exactly?" "Just here. Is there anything you can do, Doctor?" "I'll need to take a close examination, Miss." You get the idea.

Needless to say, this was not the version of my career I'd pictured. No interesting or unique cases to solve. No ground-breaking surgeries. I had to work night shifts at the Out of Hours surgery at weekends, just to make ends meet. I'd no social life and hardly saw my family. If it wasn't for getting nailed by Freddie most days, I'd have had no human contact at all, apart from the Zombie Army of patients. And my God, those patients were hard work.

It was becoming harder and harder to be civil, especially when so many of them treated me like the hired help. They'd google symptoms, come in and recite them to me. Then they'd fight me tooth and nail when I didn't agree with them or start dutifully dishing out prescriptions. That was probably the worst part of it, the total lack of respect; people treating me and the NHS like a free service to be milked for all they could get. After so many years of being a poor student, diligently trying to ace every subject, researching unusual illnesses and the newest treatments, it was soul-destroying.

That gives you some context of my frame of mind on the day Granny Green came in with three of her kids.

Granny Green was a notorious patient in the surgery, which was really saying something! She fostered local kids and could have up to four of them at any one time. She should have been lauded for her efforts, really, she should have, but she was just impossible to like. The kids always seemed to be sick, and she was constantly self-diagnosing them. She'd come in with an alphabetical list and boss the life out of us. Asthma. Autism. Appendicitis. Blocked ears. Bronchitis. It was endless. "He needs his chest listened to! Look in her ears! This one has Strep. Definitely on the spectrum is this one. I need two antibiotics, and none of that aul shite ya gave me the last time!" It went on and on.

Our working theory was, the more the kids had wrong with them, the higher the fostering allowances she received for them. I think if the kids hadn't been such a surly and bad-tempered bunch and she had been remotely civil, we wouldn't have minded trying to help her out. Instead, we hated seeing her coming and we felt bad for the kids who were stuck with her. She smelled like boiled sprouts. They all did. The kids were ashen-faced and wore tatty, mismatched hand-me-down clothes. If we brought up the subject of their diet or appearance, she'd practically roar at us, telling us to mind our own business and asking how many times we'd helped people in need out of the goodness of our hearts.

It wasn't just Granny Green's cantankerous nature that made us wary of her. We had no shortage of difficult, bad-tempered patients, and we had learned how to manage them. But she was something else; intimidating in a way that made no sense for someone of her age and stature. We had huge guys on our books, covered in tattoos spelling out the acronyms of local dodgy organisations, with their kill counts and prison sentences proudly tattooed like trophies along the length of their arms. Yet none of them were half as frightening as Granny Green.

It was rumoured that a previous GP, Dr Rogan who had co-started the surgery with Dr Johnston, took early retirement after treating her, due to a severe mental breakdown. No one was entirely sure if the story was true, or an urban myth. Hell, we were all on the verge of a mental breakdown.

The Pitbulls rotated Granny Green religiously around the surgery, so no one doctor saw her and the kids more than another. This was unusual, as continuity of care is recommended. But we were grateful for this gesture of support.

On this particular day, it was my turn.

Granny Green was ensconced in my surgery, insisting that one of her three current kids, a pale, snotty-nosed ginger lad of about eleven, needed Factor 50 suncream on prescription because of 'hyper-sensitive' skin. It was coming up to the end of the summer term, and I reckoned this really meant she didn't want to pay for any sun cream over the school holidays. I held firm. There was nothing to indicate the boy should be diagnosed with anything other than 'Irish Skin Complexion.' Admittedly, my tone probably wasn't great, and after a long argument, we ended up glaring at each other across my surgery desk while the boy in question stood to the side of her, staring at his feet and the two other boys loitered at the door.

I wasn't going to give in, and she wasn't going to leave without getting what she wanted. Stalemate.

Granny Green's eyes narrowed. "I bet you think you're all IT, sat in that chair, dearie. Eh? Wasn't an option when I was young. A woman training to be a doctor. Doctors were *men* in my day." She smiled with acid sweetness.

I bristled at the underlying inference that she'd prefer a male doctor now. "I'm pretty sure they were letting women study medicine by the time you could go to Uni, Granny. If they'd the aptitude for it."

"Oh! Would you listen to her?!" Granny Green sucked in her cheeks. "The aptitude for it. Oh! An answer for everything, this one. Is there no respect from you young ones these days?"

That pushed a button. Leaning forward, I said "I have plenty of respect for those who are genuinely in need of medical advice, Ms Green. And I'd very much like to get on and meet some of them now. So, if you don't mind." I stood and gestured to the door. She grinned slyly and leaned further back into her chair. I gritted my teeth and loomed over the desk towards her, attempting to look intimidating and authoritative.

"I bet you were always a little know-it-all. Hmm?" She continued. "Head always stuck in a book? Mum and Dad both so impressed with all the facts you could tell people? Your aptitude? Eh? Is that what you need for going to university? Not a nice family who can pay your fees? A Mum and Dad who can't believe how smart you are, eh? I bet they're so proud."

The pale boy wisely sidled off to join the other two at the door. Granny Green stood and leaned over the desk to give me a hard stare, our foreheads almost touching. Her voice dropped to a whisper. "I bet there's nothing you don't know or can't explain. Eh?" She wasn't smiling sweetly anymore. "Maybe I'll show you there's more to life than what's in your medical books."

"Goodbye, Granny Green." I practically growled.

The temperature dropped just then. I looked over to see the three boys open the door and hasten out. Was that what caused the draft? Didn't they open the door after I'd felt it? I looked back at Granny Green and recoiled back. It felt like there was *more* of Granny there than had been a minute ago. She was bigger, more solid. But it was more than that. Her eyes, her eyes were different. Bigger and darker. The room temperature dropped again, and I shuddered involuntarily.

Granny bared her teeth at me before spitting out, "You take care now, dearie. And take care of *her*. She's a needy wee thing. She doesn't like being ignored." She stood then and followed the boys out the door, smiling coldly over her shoulder as she closed the door behind her. At last glimpse of her, her eyes were back to normal.

My heart was thumping in my chest. How had she suddenly looked so threatening? Those poor kids. It took a minute before it occurred to me that I didn't know who 'her' was. Who was Granny Green talking about?

Trying to settle my nerves, I sat back in my chair, took deep breaths and looked around the room. My stomach dropped. What on earth?

In front of the bookshelf in my room, stood a tall stack of books. I stared at it in disbelief, fighting the urge to sprint out of the room.

The bookshelves and their contents had been there forever with only a few additions from me. The top shelves had old medical encyclopaedias that hadn't been opened in years. The two bottom shelves housed a range of small toys in baskets. The third shelf up was filled with children's books. There were a few larger, glossier Julia Donaldson classics which I had added but mainly the books were yellowed, smaller Enid Blyton editions that could very well have been priceless limited editions, they were so old.

Every children's book was now neatly stacked from largest to smallest. I blinked a few times, half expecting the pile to disappear. But no. A neat pile of books up to waist height remained stubbornly in front of the bookshelf. A stack that hadn't been there this morning. Hadn't been there a few minutes ago. Had it?

My heart hammered at the wrongness of it, while I replayed Granny Green's visit in my head. Had I seen any of the boys near the bookshelf? I didn't think so, but what other explanation could there be? I was still staring at the book pile when the next patient entered, already listing his symptoms and preferred medicines. I could hardly follow a word the man said. I kept glancing over to the books, willing myself to make sense of what had happened.

"Ya 'aright love? Some wee rascal been messing with your books?" He asked, exasperated at being ignored.

"What?!" I started. "No. Sorry. Please, say all that again."

God knows what I prescribed that guy, or the next lot.

I hurriedly tidied the books on my lunch break and had a stern word with myself, frustrated at letting Granny Green get under my skin. Two days later, I saw the girl.

I walked into the waiting area, and there she was, sitting with her back to me, staring at the ancient, grubby wire slide game in the middle of the waiting room, completely still. I stared at the back of her head while my patient passed me and made his own way to my surgery room. The girl was skinny with greasy brown hair, wearing a tatty, mustard pinafore over a dirty white long-sleeved top. Grubby white tights and brown leather boots completed the look. Her grimy, pale hands rested on the base of the game. She was young, but she looked old, like she'd just stepped out of a silent film. She didn't look right. She was there, but not there.

My heart raced. The waiting room was busy as usual. I looked at the other patients. They chatted, stared at their phones or rifled through tatty old copies of Heat magazine. No one else was looking at the girl. I looked back at her.

Still there.

Still not there.

Out of place and out of time.

I closed my eyes and shook my head. *Stop it. You're being ridiculous.* I chided myself.

Opening my eyes to look around the room again, I willed myself to speak. To ask if someone was with her. To check if others could see her. While I was summoning the courage, she seemed to sense my gaze and started to slowly turn her head to look at me. But it didn't look right. Her hair covered her face but, as she raised her head higher, her hair fell to the side.

Oh my God! She had no face!

Holy shit! Fear flooded through me, and I bolted down the hall to my surgery on shaking legs.

Sat in front of my patient, I tried to calm myself down. Blood was thundering in my ears so loud that I could hardly hear what they said. Surely, I was being ridiculous! The girl must have had a face. I was the problem. I had to be. I was overworked and Granny Green had got in my head.

When our session finished, I closely shadowed my patient back up the hall. He'd been after a PTSD diagnosis and strong, addictive painkillers. He was a large, steroid-taking guy who was known to be part of some local organisation. He would have been more used to people giving him a wide berth, not tailing him closely and breathing down his neck like I was. I grabbed his arm when we reached the waiting room, pulling him back to let me scan the room from over his shoulder. He gave me a bemused look.

"Someone lookin' ya, love?" he asked sardonically.

In that part of Belfast, if you had *'someone lookin' ya,'* it didn't mean they wanted to return the tenner they owed you. More likely you were in for a kneecapping or a beating. Or both.

"Er, No... Just checking..." I scanned the waiting room, still gripping his arm.

"Uhuh. In that case, if ya don' mind, love." He looked pointedly at my hand on his arm and then back up at my face.

"Yep! All good. Ha!" I let go of him and didn't even feel annoyed about being called 'love' instead of Doctor, a pet peeve of mine. I shouted manically for my next patient, who, judging by the look on their face, clearly wished the Pitbulls had assigned them a different Doctor. *Get a Grip,* I chided myself.

Anyone can rationalise a weird sighting as the person being overwrought or as it being just plain wrong. That's what I told myself.

I'd seen a real girl with a real face. Maybe she had a flesh-coloured balaclava on, part of a skin treatment or something. No supernatural explanation needed. *She had a face,* I repeated to myself. She definitely, absolutely had a face.

Over a fortnight went by, and I'd almost shaken the experience off. So, when I left my surgery reading a file one evening and looked up to see the girl ahead of me in the corridor, looking up at me with baleful eyes, I almost had a heart attack. Hand on heart, I willed myself to calm down. What was wrong with me? If I was seeing a girl, then a girl was there.

“Hi,” I said in a shaky voice, forcing myself to look at her. She slowly raised a hand to wave at me and, at that moment, I looked her up and down properly.

In a heart stopping moment, I realised she had no legs!

She was dressed in the same pinafore outfit as before, but there was nothing beneath the hem of her dress. She was floating in mid-air. Everything spun as I looked up from where her legs should have been to her face.

She smiled widely.

I screamed loudly.

She moved towards me, and I threw the file in the air and ran back into my surgery, slamming and locking the door.

My phone rang almost instantly, and I shakily grabbed the receiver. “What’s happening?!” Freddie demanded from the surgery beside mine.

We had clear procedures on what to do if or when one of the patients ‘kicked off.’ We had a small number of severely mentally ill patients who really should have been committed, and a large number of drug-dependent, dangerous patients who really should have been locked up. The protocols for dealing with incidents were drummed into us: lock yourself in your surgery and call for help. Don't be a hero.

"WHAT'S HAPPENING, SARAH?!" Freddie roared, when I didn't answer immediately.

What was I going to say? There's a ghost in the corridor? "Nothing! Nothing. I slammed the door by accident." I stammered.

"You what?" Freddie hung up and barged round to my door, pounding it rudely. "What is going on?" He hissed when I opened the door. I cautiously put my head out in the corridor. To my right, Freddie's elderly patient was gawping warily at me from Freddie's door, one hand nervously clutching the top of her cardigan. I forced myself to look to the left, to where I'd seen the girl. There was no one there. "Nothing. Sorry, I didn't mean to scare you, Freddie."

"Nothin'? You look like you've seen a ghost."

That made me laugh.

Again, I blamed stress and being overworked. I must have imagined she had no legs. Of course she had bloody legs!

There are no such things as ghosts. I'd repeat, repeat, repeat to myself. I was a woman of science for fuck's sake!

A week later, one Sunday night after a bottle of wine to quash the Sunday doom, I decided that if I saw the girl again, I'd stand my ground, call someone, and prove she was either real, or that I needed a psychiatric evaluation. I'd hoped I'd have a few weeks to work up the courage. But the very next day, I'd gone to the waiting room to help an elderly patient with mobility issues with the walk down to my surgery. I spotted the girl in the waiting room again, sitting with her back to me, staring up at the window.

I scanned around the room. No one was looking at the girl. That doesn't mean they can't see her, I rationalised. Still looking at her, I saw her shift slightly. I knew that she knew I was watching her.

Heart thumping, I took a deep breath. "Who is with this young lady?" I asked loudly, getting everyone's attention.

As one, the people in the room looked at me, then looked around the room. I looked back at the girl. She'd swivelled right around to face me and with relief I saw her face looked normal. Albeit a bit dirty, with a sly, challenging grin. 'What now?' her look implied.

I swallowed hard, fear rising. My mouth dried. "This girl, here!" I said again, even louder, and gestured to where she sat.

Everyone looked uncomfortable. They started making eyes at each other. In desperation, I looked to the reception area. Both Pitbulls were slowly shaking their heads at me. Why? Was the girl not there? Or were they warning me to stop?

I looked back towards the girl and cried out. She was standing now and had moved impossibly close to me without me seeing her move in my peripheral vision. No one else was looking at her. They were all watching me.

I glanced to the Pitbulls again. "What?" I hissed at them. They were stock still now, their wide eyes glued to me. "Go!" Pitbull one mouthed. "Now!"

Without looking at the girl again, I offered my arm to the elderly patient and helped him down to my surgery, my cheeks burning with frustration and embarrassment, and my heart pounding with fear. I didn't stop shaking for half an hour.

There was no denying it after that. I was seeing a ghost. I'd spy her at least two or three times a week. My nerves were shot, but somehow, I held it together. I avoided the girl as best I could, and I survived the surgery by taking it one day and one patient at a time. I walked the patients to and from the surgery, so I wasn't alone in the corridor with her, and, thankfully, she kept her distance.

During it all, my encounters with Freddie were welcome distractions. There was no pretence of love, just lots of pleasure. This was fucking, not love-making. The orgasms reminded me I was alive, and the post coital comedown calmed my nerves. When it was just us in the surgery after hours, I stuck to him like glue, and he usually offered to lock up. If he noticed any changes in me, he was either polite enough not to say, or he simply didn't care enough to bring it up.

The girl was in the waiting room one morning when Granny Green was waiting to see one of the other doctors. She looked at me when I was calling for another patient and cocked an eyebrow in the girl's direction, smiling sweetly. Oh, that bitch saw her alright!

I'd almost forgotten it all started with Granny Green. I finished with my patient and let them see themselves out. I wasn't massively behind on appointment times and decided to have a quick peek in Granny Green's e-file. This wasn't strictly allowed, as she wasn't my patient that day. There were, still are, strict rules about reviewing files belonging to patients you aren't directly treating. Auditing teams can track your search histories and ask for verification that they are all your patients. But, as Granny Green attended the *surgery* that, I decided it was pretty low risk.

Maureen Patricia Green was her actual name, and she was only fifty-six! Jesus, she looked seventy easy! I went back about five years, but there was nothing of note. She'd been with us forever, so her notes were too extensive for a quick read between patients. And I knew the likelihood of me finding anything that could help me was slim.

Then, and I am ashamed to admit this, I looked up the medical records of the GP, Dr Rogan, who was rumoured to have been medically retired after treating Granny Green a few decades ago. I went and dug her paper file out of the archives one evening while Freddie was occupied elsewhere.

My stomach sank as I read it. She'd displayed increasingly erratic behaviour in work before going off on long-term sick. The phrase 'Paranoid Delusions' came up a lot. Schizophrenia was suspected. There had been some success with treatment at home before the paranoia came back with a bang, and she was sectioned in a secure ward for a number of months. She never returned to work.

I knew I was making huge leaps, but the thought of the poor doctor being haunted here, before being haunted at home, before being locked up, terrified me. What if the girl had followed her to the secure ward as well? The poor woman.

And, selfishly, was this my future? Is that how people would describe me? Of having 'Paranoid Delusions' of seeing a girl in the waiting room? I steeled my nerves, determined I wouldn't end up with the same fate. The Doctor who had treated Dr Rogan, was, of course, Dr Johnston.

There was no avoiding it, I was going to have to ask the old bastard for help.

Later that day, I stopped at reception and told the Pitbulls I needed them to schedule some time for me to meet with Dr Johnston. Pitbull Two stared up at me under her fake eyelashes with such a sceptical expression you'd have thought I'd asked her to arrange an audience with the Pope for me.

"Wha' fur?" She asked in her broad Belfast accent.

Irritated by her attitude, I reminded myself I was the doctor and she the receptionist, so technically, she worked for me. Firmly, I said, "It's a private matter. Just plan the appointment." She blinked slowly at me twice, not moving a muscle.

I sighed in frustration. "I need advice on a patient."

"Who an' advice about wha?" She replied in a bored tone.

"Does it matter?" I snapped.

"Yea. Matters." She deadpanned with another slow blink.

"It's in relation to Granny Green, if you must know." I answered tersely.

The two Pitbulls swivelled their heads in sync, to lock eyes each other with raised eyebrows.

"Leave it with us." Pitbull One said, before turning back to her screen, effectively dismissing me.

I stalked off without thanking them. The next day as I passed reception with a cup of tea, Pitbull One blurted, "Ten o'clock. Twenty minutes."

It took me a second to work out what she meant. "I've to meet Dr Johnston at ten o'clock for twenty minutes?" I replied.

"No flies on you." She confirmed, without looking up from her screen.

I forced myself to say, "Thanks." Then I went to my office to figure out what I was going to say and ask. I mean I couldn't tell him what was going on. I'd have to be creative. At ten o'clock, I practically ejected a rambling patient and made my way to Dr Johnston's surgery, knocking lightly on the door before entering.

Dr Johnston was leaning back in his chair, arms folded over his large stomach. He eyed me as I entered without speaking or inviting me to sit. Nervously, I lowered myself into the chair in front of his desk.

He raised his eyebrows. "Well?" He asked, not altogether unpleasantly.

Losing my nerve by the minute, I mumbled, "Um, I need some advice on how to treat Granny Green and, er, one of her kids."

"Which is it?" He asked, again not entirely unfriendly in his manner. "Help with Granny Green or help with one of her kids?"

I faltered. What was I thinking? What could I possibly say? What questions would get me answers? Abandoning this as a bad idea, I said "Granny Green. She says one of her prescriptions has stopped working but I don't know what else to prescribe that won't affect the efficacy of her other prescriptions."

Dr Johnston and I stared at each other for a long moment as my blatant lie hung in the air like a bad smell. My toes curled with embarrassment as the silence continued.

"Well, that's a relief," he said, eventually. "For a minute there I thought I was going to have another colleague tell me a little ghost girl was following them around the surgery."

My eyes widened like balloons. His jaw flexed and he broke our gaze to look up at the ceiling. Appalled, I realised his eyes had welled up. *What did he know*?

"Was it Dr Rogan who told you about a ghost girl?" I asked, my voice thick with emotion.

"Yes." He answered, clearly struggling with a lump in his throat. With an effort, he cleared his throat and visibly tried to pull himself together. "Dr Rogan was an exceptional Doctor. They don't make them like her anymore." He added as an afterthought, casting a withering glance my way. Ah yes, there's the Dr Johnston we all know and love.

He paused, as if unable to continue.

"Can you tell me about what happened?" I pressed.

Dr Johnston rolled his eyes. But it seemed more in exasperation than derision. Moments passed. I wondered if he was going to ask me to leave.

"Granny Green was a real problem round here when Dr Rogan and I opened this surgery in the late sixties. She was well known in the community as a 'healer.' When it wasn't the norm to have births in hospital, women often called upon her to help with home births and, by all accounts, she was a good midwife."

"She also 'bought' people's ailments off them. Warts, acne, carbuncles, eczema and the like would only cost you a few pence and a surprising amount of people found the payments worked. They'd pay her to cure hands covered in warts that they'd spent years trying to rid themselves of. A few days later, they'd be washing their hands with soap and every wart would come off and be washed away."

"We had patients come in to crow that we hadn't helped them in all the years they'd been coming to us, but Granny Green had cured them in a matter of days. They thought we should send people to her! We didn't believe a word of it but, often, we couldn't explain the results. When Granny Green came in for herself and the foster kids, she made a big point of telling us we were a last resort, only used for things beyond her abilities or for the free medicines. God, she was hateful, even then."

But a lot of people looked up to her. That's what made her dangerous. Her reputation was good. It inspired people to go to her for help with things beyond her supposed 'abilities.' Abortions. Infections. New lumps. Changes in moles. Things that needed modern medicine, not gypsy cures and snake oil. Her ego drove her to deter people coming to us. She'd spread rumours of malpractice."

"The education system wasn't what it is now, or social services for that matter, so many young mothers were particularly vulnerable to her promises, as they knew no better. One young unwed mother was her undoing."

Dr Johnston paused to swallow; pain etched on his face.

"It was a few years after the surgery had opened when a young mother brought her ten-year-old daughter to Granny Green, seeking help for persistent stomach pain. The mother was only twenty-five, forced out of school early by her own pregnancy. Uneducated, she was an easy mark for Granny Green."

"Granny Green told her that if she took the girl to our surgery, we'd call social services and accuse her of neglect. She spun her usual lies: that rich families wanted young girls for maids, and doctors helped supply them by funnelling children from unwed mothers into foster care. With her own family having disowned her, the mother had no one else to turn to."

"All of this came out later, in court, after the girl died."

"It was the poor girl's neighbour who finally recognised the danger. She'd gone round to complain about hearing the child crying all night. One look at the girl was enough. She bundled mother and daughter into her car and drove them straight to us. Dr Rogan took one glance, diagnosed a burst appendix, and called the ambulance."

"They did everything they could, but sepsis was inevitable at that late stage. It was a terrible death. One that shocked the neighbourhood and made the papers."

"The locals turned on Granny Green then. The neighbour who'd tried to save the girl was a formidable woman herself. She had Granny Green's windows put in and graffiti daubed on her house. People were encouraged to come forward with their stories about when Granny Green's cures had let them down. Fathers had been lost to cancer because of late diagnosis. Expectant mothers who had been told to avoid doctors, resulting in traumatic and dangerous births that could easily have been avoided. So much claptrap nonsense."

"It was a strange time, back then people didn't want to bother Doctors or go to hospital unless they were gravely ill. Granny Green wasn't the only 'healer' who ruled the roost in some of the more deprived areas."

"After the girl died, the police became involved, of course. But it was a tricky case. To all who knew her, Granny Green was the obvious culprit, but it was the girl's mother who hadn't sought medical help for her daughter who was ultimately blamed.

She was charged with neglect. The night before her trial was due to start..."

Dr Johnston stopped, tears now flowing down his ruddy cheeks. Continuing with difficulty he said, "Do you know, Sarah, I've seen so much - too much in this job. But that mother is the one who still breaks my heart. Still gives me nightmares."

Please stop, I begged silently. *I don't want to know.*

Dr Johnston continued, not bothering to wipe the tears.

"The night before her trial, the mother walked to Granny Green's with a petrol can in one hand a lighter in the other."

"She called to Granny Green from the garden, attracting attention from neighbours as she did so. Granny Green came to the window. Calmly, by all accounts, the mother lifted the petrol can and tipped it over her head. People poured out of their houses. Running. Screaming. Begging her to stop. She didn't and before anyone could reach her, she self-immolated. The fire was so intense that there was nothing anyone could do."

"My God! We treated patients who'd witnessed it for years afterwards. So, we had to keep reliving it too. There was an inquest into the mother's death and Granny Green was investigated as part of it but nothing came of it. The mother was a troubled young woman, unloved and unvalued. No one vouched for her. People were embarrassed to corroborate how respected Granny Green had been."

"As she was the one who treated the girl, it was Dr Rogan who gave evidence in court. And oh, did she go to town on Granny Green. Fuelled by outrage on what had transpired, she didn't hold back. But all for naught."

"On the stand, Granny Green said she'd begged the mother to take her daughter to hospital and believed she was getting medical help. Granny Green was just trying to 'give some comfort' and 'keep an eye on the girl.' All lies, of course, but manslaughter was always going to be tough to prove, especially with all Granny Green's fostering work and the key witness, the mother, being dead. No one could say for sure what had passed between them."

"Granny Green was not found guilty, although the Judge had the good grace to acknowledge that this did not mean she was innocent."

"Time passed and to our amazement, after a short break, Granny Green was back fostering. No conviction, no reason not to, eh? And she didn't even have the good grace to move surgeries, so we had to keep treating her. She would only take appointments with Dr Rogan, having an almost uncanny ability to book in when I was on leave or busy elsewhere. Dr Rogan could barely be civil to her."

"And then, sightings of the girl started. After visits from Granny Green, Dr Rogan would see the girl in the surgery, still dressed in the tatty mustard pinafore she was wearing the day she arrived here with the neighbour. At first, she saw her intermittently, and she said the girl wasn't always 'whole.' I never really knew what she meant by that, if I'm being honest."

I think I know, I answered inwardly, remembering the girl's missing face and legs.

"And then the sightings increased in both intensity and frequency. That's when Dr Rogan came to me for help. Naturally, I thought the sightings were the result of mental fatigue. Treating a child too far gone with appendicitis is a particularly stressful event. Add on the hideous death of the mother and the subsequent court case, never mind living and working in Northern Ireland in the early seventies, it was a wonder she functioned at all."

"But, as I said, Dr Rogan was a remarkable woman. The sightings were her only symptom, which didn't tally for someone whose mental wellbeing had deteriorated enough to cause hallucinations. We ran every test of course, brain scans, psychiatric evaluations, the works. She aced them all. But the sightings continued."

"They started at home as well as here. The girl started communicating with her, whispering in her ear at night. Terrible things. Asking why she hadn't saved her. No matter that Dr Rogan had done her best for the girl, this was not a benevolent spirit. She saw the girl so frequently, well, it would wear anyone down." Dr Johnston stopped then, seemingly finished."

"What happened?" I asked eventually, panicking that this was all the information I would get.

Dr Johnston turned to look at me. "Eventually, it broke her and I had to recommend she be sectioned for her own wellbeing."

"She had become suicidal?" I asked.

"Yes. Thank God the spell in the institution stopped the sightings, and she was able to slowly rebuild her life. But returning to the surgery wasn't feasible for her by then. Dr Rogan had received the best of treatment, but instinct told us both it was the prolonged separation from Granny Green that really made the difference." He leaned towards me, then took off his glasses and gave me a hard stare. "Tell me Sarah, why you? What did you do that started all this?"

I thought back to the day Granny Green and I had argued over the sunscreen. "She told me she couldn't have become a doctor back in her day, as only men could do it. I said that wasn't true, she just didn't have the aptitude for it."

Dr Johnston snorted so loudly I thought he was choking. But no, I just hadn't heard the man laugh before. "Oh, the ego on that old crone. Yes, I bet that was it. Did you give her the prescriptions she was after?"

"No. She was talking crap, and I refused." I confirmed.

More snorting. "Yes, I'd say that could do it. A young doctor she's no respect for not only refuses to dole out the medicine on her shopping list but also tells her she was too thick to have become a doctor herself. Ha!" Dr Johnston leaned back and looked at me with something close to respect.

"What do I do now?" I asked.

"How the hell would I know? I studied at Queens too, not bloody Hogwarts!" He snapped.

Oh, for God's sake.

Dr Johnston sighed deeply, and his face softened a little. "But... if I *were* to offer any advice on matters relating to, er, Granny Green..." he answered in a softer tone, clearly being careful not to say, 'matters of the supernatural,' "...it would be this. Granny Green's power always came from fear. Spreading fear of doctors and modern medicine. Fear that if you sought help elsewhere and it didn't work, she wouldn't help you when you slunk back with your tail between your legs. Fear that if you didn't take her advice, things would deteriorate and you'd have to live with the consequences."

"Don't forget, it wasn't only people like the unfortunate young mother who fell under her spell. Well educated patients I'd treated for years could be convinced to pay her a visit for something they wanted a quick fix for, then I'd not see them for months, years even. And, as much as it pains me to admit it, sometimes people were healed by her in ways I could not explain. It's something that vexes me terribly. It pains me to say it, but there is something about Granny Green you couldn't put your finger on. I wouldn't want to meet her in a dark alley, that's all I'll say." Dr Johnston stood then.

"That's it?" I asked.

"Yes. That's all I'll say. Did you not hear me?" He answered in his usual dismissive tone and gestured to the door. "Don't you have patients waiting? Don't think I'll be seeing them just because you ran over our twenty minutes."

I left his surgery in a daze, realising almost an hour had passed. I skipped lunch to catch up, but wrote down what Dr Johnston had told me that evening, memorising every word.

And after? The girl kept popping up, in various states of wholeness. Mostly she was in the waiting room, or the hallways. It's truly amazing what you can learn to live with.

Until the night things blew up.

Freddie and I were going at it hammer and tongs one Friday evening in his surgery. I was sitting on the bed, legs wrapped around his waist, hands round his neck as he stood in front of me, thrusting with his back to the door. Over his shoulder, the door had been left open, and I could see up the hall towards reception. Some movement caught my eye, and I glanced over his shoulder, where I saw the door of his surgery start to swing slowly over.

Oh my God. It was her! In the room with us.

I watched in horror as she slowly pushed the door closed, closing us in the room with her. Terror flooded me.

"Freddie! Freddie!" I tried to whisper-shout in panic, as I squeezed my hand into his neck.

"Oh, yeah, nearly there," he panted back, holding me tighter and speeding up.

I could see her clearly now. Her face was sullen. Defiant. Angry. She no longer looked like a pathetic wee urchin. She looked terrifying. And she was staring right at me.

"Freddie!" I said, louder, hitting the back of his head.

"Uh huh, you there yet?"

"No, Freddie!" I shouted and pushed him back, shoving him out of me.

"What the fuck?" He shouted back indignantly, hand on his cock.

"Look!" I hissed and pointed.

Freddie turned, leapt in the air with fright, and let out the highest-pitched scream I've ever heard in my life from a human being. "Wah!" Honestly, I wouldn't have thought it possible for a man to hit such high notes if I hadn't heard it in person. Then, the bastard yanked up his trousers, darted out the door and sprinted up the hall, still shrieking like a slapped soprano.

I stood by the surgery bed, heart pounding, staring at the girl. She stared back, insolently. Panic and revulsion came in waves. I thought I was going to faint. I was absolutely fucking petrified. Isn't it 'Flight, Fight or Freeze'? Freddie had fled alright. But I was frozen in horror.

Moments passed as the girl stood, motionless, staring at me.

And then? Then the adrenaline started to abate as I looked at her and nothing happened. Neither of us moved. A few more moments passed. I took a deep breath in. Then, I took a small step towards her. She shimmered just a little. I looked down. Her legs had disappeared again.

I took another small step towards her, staring at her intently. A strange calmness came over me. I closed my eyes and broke our gaze, shoved down my skirt and walked briskly up the corridor before bursting out of the front door into the carpark.

Freddie was there, hyperventilating beside a wall. "WHAT THE ACTUAL FUCK?!" He managed to screech between breaths.

Whew. Where to start? "Come on, I'll buy you a pint."

Thankfully, he had his keys in his pocket, and we were able to lock the front door and leave without having to go back inside. I drove his car to a pub near where he lived and told him everything as he gulped down four or five pints and a few whiskey chasers. He didn't take the story well. In fact, he was so freaked out that he insisted I stay with him that night, as he didn't want to be alone.

Do not be thinking this was the start of some actual romance blossoming. The drunker he got, the more he took thick with me for 'knowingly putting him in danger.' He huffed and stomped around the house all evening, getting more and more belligerent, before making me sleep on his sofa despite having two spare rooms with comfy looking beds. I scarpered early the next day.

The rest of the weekend passed slowly with anxiety eating at my insides. For a start, Freddie and I hadn't cleared up after ourselves on Friday evening. My knickers and handbag were in his surgery. Not the sort of detail the Pitbull receptionists or Dr Johnston would miss, or ignore. I could have called into the surgery on the Saturday or Sunday to clear up, of course. But the fear of the dead girl haunting the office trumped the fear of the Pitbulls discovering I was shagging Freddie. Who was I kidding? No doubt they already knew, omniscient bitches.

I slunk in sheepishly early on Monday morning, head down, nodding with as much dignity as I could muster to Dr Johnston and the Pitbulls as I passed them on the way to my surgery. The first thing I saw was my handbag, sitting primly on my table. As I went around the table to get to my chair, I spied my underwear. Laid out neatly on my seat.

Fucking brilliant.

I shoved the knickers in the bag, heart pounding and sat down. Thankfully, there was no sign of the girl. But then Pitbull Two terrorised me more than the ghost girl ever could, by entering the office with a cup of tea. She'd brought me tea. To my office. For me! This was unheard of!

She sat the tea on my desk. I blinked at her, mouth agape. She stood still, smiling kindly. I swallowed nervously. She stopped smiling at me. My heart sank.

Dear God, what was coming? Was she sacking me? Could she do that? Probably.

In a terrifyingly kind tone, she said, "It's hard. I know. Especially at first if you're not used to them. But she's not *really here*, you know? You'll be alright. Just keep doing what you're good at. Oh, and Himself's called in sick. Men, eh?" Then she smiled again and left.

I don't know how long I sat in stunned silence. I was right, she had seen the girl in the waiting room. I yelped when the buzzer went off to indicate a patient was on their way down. Then I pulled myself together and got on with my day. Doing what I was good at. Belatedly, I realised she'd paid me a compliment.

The day passed uneventfully. I tried and failed to avoid Dr Johnston. But he mustn't have been told what happened, as he didn't bring it up, and there was no way he'd have ignored an opportunity to embarrass me.

That evening, I called over to Freddie's. He didn't answer the door. Guessing he hadn't left the house since the evening of the incident, I returned with his favourite take-away and sat outside calling him on my mobile and ringing his doorbell until I wore him down and he reluctantly let me in. I guessed right, he'd been living on out-of-date Super Noodles from the back of his cupboards. He wolfed down the food I'd brought, and we talked late into the evening. He returned to work the next morning.

A week or so later Dr Johnston deigned to poke his nose into my office, disdainfully scanning the room as he asked, "Everything alright?"

"You saw her, didn't you? The girl." I replied.

"What?" He said, in a tone that implied I'd just asked what his favourite sex position was.

"The girl. You saw her too. There's no way you'd believe Dr Rogan if you hadn't." I replied, loudly.

"Well, I never." He replied in an outraged tone. "You try to help, and it's all thrown back at you. Bloody new generation...blah blah blah" As he walked off down the hall.

But I had him pegged. No wonder he only worked two days a week. I felt for him; he'd had a tough old time of it. But it was no excuse for the laziness, cheekiness and lack of help he gave, especially for the money he was on. I wasn't putting up with his shitty attitude anymore.

Things just continued to tick on after that. Occasionally, I saw the girl. She still scared the wits out of me, but I could handle it. I stood my ground each time she appeared, and she seemed less whole each time.

Strangely, I felt better. Stronger somehow. Like I'd faced a lion and survived.

So, when Pitbull Two, or Barbara as I'd started calling her by then, rang to apologetically say Granny Green was en route, I didn't panic. I knew they'd protected me from her for as long as they could.

"Granny Green! It's been a while. How are you? Take a seat. On your own today, I see." I welcomed her, smiling widely. She didn't answer. Instead, she took her time to settle into the seat opposite me and looked at me cooly. I waited, still smiling.

"Well dearie. Never mind me. How have *you* been lately?" She said in a faux friendly tone.

"Me? Not bad at all, Granny. Not bad at all." I smiled tightly.

"Is that right, dearie?"

"That's right, Granny."

She eyed me closely. The air changed, charged somehow. The temperature in the room dropped. From the corner of my eye, I could just see the bed.

A sort of shadow formed over it. A wave of unease swept over me. The hairs on my arms raised up and I stole a glance over to the bed when I opened Granny Green's file. The shadow formed the shape of a small person.

It was the girl. In the room with us. My stomach lurched, and I balled my hands into fists under the table. Would she be more whole with Granny Green here? I thought of the whispering Dr Rogan spoke of. Please no.

"Nothing new to report? Eh, dearie?" Granny Green said cheerfully, a smug grimace on her face that made me want to reach over and smack her.

I saw the girl move to the edge of the bed.

How was she doing this?!

"All is well, Granny Green. All is well." Adrenaline pumped through me. I wanted to vomit. I held her gaze.

My heart pounded in my chest as I sensed the girl slide languidly off the bed. Panic rising, I could feel her coming closer, moving slowly but steadily towards me. She lifted her arm towards me.

Granny Green leaned forward, smiling conspiratorially and said in a hushed tone, "I do hope she hasn't caused you any bother, dearie." She jutted her chin in the direction of the girl. "She can be a clingy wee thing. I should know."

The girl was within touching distance of my shoulder now. I shuddered and leaned forward, making eye contact with the hateful old crone in front of me.

"I'm not sure I know what you mean, Granny. There's no one else here."

We stared hard at each other, no love lost.

"You've not been seeing things, have you Granny? Is that why you're in today? I sure hope not. I'd feel just terrible if I had to report you as being mentally unfit to keep fostering. And you in the prime of your life an' all. Sure, who would boil the sprouts for the children then?"

Granny Green's eyes flashed with hatred and bitterness.

So did mine.

I could feel the icy chill from the girl's hand, hovering over my shoulder now.

FUCK YOU! I screamed silently at Granny Green as we glared at each other.

How *dare you make my life harder than it already is! You hate-filled old bitch.*

She's not really here. Barbara's words echoed in my ears. I closed my eyes and summoned all the courage I could.

She's. Not. Really. Here.

Do. It. Now!

Slowly, I turned my head to face the girl directly. My eyes bored into the side of her head, while she stared at Granny Green. Then…she shimmered a little; flickered once and disappeared completely.

The air changed, the coldness abating immediately.

I inhaled deeply, calming my nerves. I turned back to Granny Green and leaned back, triumphant. "See, Granny? I'm the only one you need to worry about here."

Granny Green shot me a look of pure poison, before looking around the room angrily, mouth gaping.

Then she stood and left without another word.

Chapter 5

The Gathering, 19:40

Sarah beams as she generously refills her wine glass.

"And that, as they say, was that! And d'ya know, it was the kick up the arse I needed to change my life. I was done with the surgery, done with Freddie. I spotted a training opportunity on the maternity wards a few weeks later, applied for it, and to my utter shock, got it! It was, thanks in no small way due to a glowing reference from Dr Johnston, which helped blow the other candidates out of the water. I could only surmise that Barbara wrote it for me, as the old bastard would never have even replied to a reference request.

I saw the girl a couple of times after that, but she'd sort of faded, like an old photograph. I could see through her and couldn't feel her presence as much as before. All the fear had gone and I ended up viewing her with pity. Barbara and I have stayed friends to this day, but we've never mentioned the girl, so I don't know if she's still there. These things are just too hard to talk about. And she won't admit to writing my reference. God that saved me. I really owe her for that. Imagine if I was still stuck in that practice! Poor Freddie still is."

Ameera laughs and smiles at Sarah with obvious admiration. "Sarah is far too modest to say she's now one of the most respected Obstetricians in the island of Ireland, so I'll say it for her. She's fantastic! She gets all the complicated cases that everyone else is scared to take on. Hear, hear!"

Taking Ameera's lead, we all raise our glasses to Sarah, muttering affirmations. Sarah covers her eyes theatrically in mock coyness.

"Ameera! You make it sound so glamorous. By 'complicated,' she means I look after all the emergency C-Sections that make the student doctors pass out and regret not becoming GPs. If only they knew the perils of local surgery!" Everyone roars with laughter at that, apart from me. I realise the others are quite tipsy by now, having knocked back a fair amount of wine already with only the finger food to sustain them.

Eleanor leans over the table towards Sarah, arms folded under her huge bosom, a radiant look of excitement on her face. "I love this story, but it wrecks my head! Could Granny Green just latch the wee girl on whoever she wanted? Where was she when she wasn't with you?"

"And why could you, Freddie, Dr Johnston and the receptionists see her when the others couldn't?" adds Joanna.

"And what happened to the poor old GP, Dr Rogan?" asks LA excitedly. "Did you ever go and visit her?"

"Oh, I don't think Sarah's one encounter makes her an expert, now does it?" Lydia says softly, making air quotes on the word encounter.

Yeesh. What a cow!

Sarah's jaw drops, and her face twists into a scowl. The tension in the room is palpable. Everyone looks at her expectantly. She's twisting her black polo neck under her chin with one hand, the other balled into a fist on the table.

"Just 'cause most of us only had one encounter, while you saw ghosts all your life, doesn't mean you've got a bloody monopoly..."

LA cuts across her. "I thought these Gatherings were supposed to be supportive, Lydia?" she says pointedly.

"Yes, of course. And I am supportive of what you *think* you saw. I just don't think we should ignore alternative explanations, where there are any." Lydia answers in a calm, patronising tone.

"What? Like me actually being mad?" LA snarls at her.

"Well we weren't talking about you, LA. But I'm sure the many, many doctors and psychiatrists you were treated by didn't call you mad when they diagnosed you." Lydia answers in the same light tone, seemingly oblivious to the ire she's causing. She doesn't fool me.

At this moment, you can cut the air with a knife. I look at Joanna. She looks upset. What's up with Lydia, trying to ruin the lovely evening Joanna has put together for everyone?

"Excuse me, Sarah?" I say, nervously. Everyone stops glaring at Lydia and turns to look at me.

"Yes?!" Sarah snaps, fury still contorting her face.

"Did you never see anything else? Like at the hospital? Or on the wards?" I trail off, hating how thin my voice sounds. I squirm in my seat. "You know, I just thought, if you were going to see a ghost anywhere, it might be in a place where lots of people...die? Like...a hospital." I elaborate, embarrassment rising.

LA and Eleanor make eyes at each other. I want to slap them. Are we not supposed to ask questions? Are we meant to just sit and listen politely to the stories? Maybe Joanna could text me the flipping etiquette next time.

Sarah visibly calms before answering thoughtfully, "A few times, I thought I might have seen something. But nothing as solid as that girl in the GP surgery became. Mind you, some of the hospital staff have stories that would turn your hair white. But it's hard to separate what's genuine from what's a good story."

"Indeed!" says Lydia, unnecessarily.

Sarah turns to her furiously.

"Right!" Joanna shouts, making me jump in my seat. "Food! Now! Grab a plate, everyone."

Ameera, Lydia and I stand and shuffle awkwardly over to the kitchen island. LA and Sarah sit whispering angrily, glancing at Lydia. Joanna hurriedly sets out pots and trays of delicious-smelling food, shooing away all offers of help. Chilli con carne, fragrant rice, spiced potatoes, naan breads, guacamole, sour cream, fresh coriander and lime wedges soon jostle for space. We politely serve ourselves before milling about eating it around the breakfast bar. Everything tastes amazing. We all murmur compliments, but Joanna waves her hands to shush us, saying it's nothing, just a simple chilli. She looks flustered and, without eating, goes to the hall and up the stairs.

I stand close to Ameera and catch her looking at me again with that same pitying stare. I smile awkwardly and lean towards her, aiming to start a conversation. She curtly turns her head and pointedly starts up a conversation with Lydia instead. Charming!

I eat quietly, watching the friends gossip tipsily with their mouths full. So, two stories down from LA and Sarah. I wonder who'll be next. Will they all take a turn? I start worrying again that they'll want me to tell a story. I've cleaned in a few places in my time that would give you the willies. Empty dentist's offices and empty schools after hours could have you jumping at shadows. But nothing scary has ever actually happened, and, truth be told, I don't believe in ghosts.

I don't think revealing that particular fact will go down well with this crowd.

But who could ever be sure? Do ghosts exist, and have these women genuinely seen and experienced them and been injured by them? Or do they not exist, and the women are either making all this up, or, turning a few bad but explainable experiences into an elaborate plot, like Lydia seems to think? Goodness knows.

The chilli is hot, and I gulp more of the delicious rosé wine to cool my tongue. I clear my plate and eye up the leftovers. My cupboards are bare at home. I've overspent on an unexpected bill this month, and I'm waiting on a few cash-in-hand jobs later this week before I can go food shopping again. Joanna's is one of them.

I briefly wonder if there is any chance she would pay me in advance, but I'd rather die than ask her for money in front of this lot. However, if there is a doggy bag going, I certainly won't refuse. And I know someone else who'd appreciate them. Meanwhile, I pile my plate with a second helping and refill my glass. May as well get my money's worth while I'm here, especially as I still have no clue why I've been included.

The women continue to ignore me as they eat. Often, when I clean or serve at events, it's as if I've just become part of the furniture, as likely to be spoken to as a standing lamp. My name scares people too. I have an Irish Mam and an English Dad. Mam overcompensated for the English in me by giving me an obscure Irish name most Northerners have never heard of. Hell, most Irish don't know it either. I always have to repeat it a few times before people will even attempt it, their mouths twitching like cat butts while they try to form the first syllable. Mw, Mw, Mw.

I grew up in Dundalk but when I left school, I moved to Belfast. I thought it would be cheaper to live and easier to find work here. The few 'proper' job interviews I'd gone to had been so excruciatingly painful that I just gave up on looking for permanent work and focussed on seeking out decent-paying temp roles. Cleaning, waitressing, litter picking, concert security, dog walking, Christmas shelf stocking, Post Office elf... you name it, I did it. And it wasn't like I was overqualified for them, having left school with mediocre Leaving Cert results.

I have enough semi-regular 'official' roles to cover most of my bills, and I clean rich people's private homes for cash in hand to live off. The rich pay more per hour than the temp jobs, and the owners often make nicer bosses.

Joanna McCann is a case in point. I think she's a Life Coach but styles herself as a therapist. She is always poised to dish out advice and guidance, whether you want it or not. I imagine she spends her days telling other fabulous women how great they are while they worry that their lives don't have meaning. She's usually glowing. But she has a nervous energy this evening, which is strange given she's surrounded by old friends in her beautiful home, serving delicious food at her 'edgy' themed party. Maybe she's had bad news about her sister but didn't want to cancel the party.

I know Joanna's sister has been unwell, but I'm unsure what her illness is. I don't like to press for details when they aren't offered, and Joanna clearly finds it hard to talk about her. Leukaemia, cancer or something is my guess as, according to Joanna, she is getting a lot of treatment without getting any better. When Joanna comes back downstairs, she looks tired. She joins in conversation with Lydia and Ameera. I can hear Lydia asking how her sister is doing. Joanna shakes her head at Lydia while she updates her, and Lydia wears a sad, sympathetic expression. I guess there isn't any improvement.

"So...how are you enjoying the night so far?" Eleanor sidles up and asks me, just as I shovel a huge forkful into my mouth. Embarrassed, I flap my hand at my mouth to indicate I can't answer while I frantically chew, mouth on fire.

"Isn't the chipotle chilli *fantastic*? Joanna's such a good cook. I must get the recipe. What did you think of the first two stories?" Eleanor asks.

"M'huh." I answer, still chewing.

"It was a good idea of Joanna's to include you. We're all friends with Joanna, but as you can see from the little bitchy twosome huffing at the table," she pauses to gesture to LA and Sarah who have retreated back to the dining table, "we aren't always the *best* of friends. Lydia can be challenging. Nice when you get to know her, but she doesn't suffer fools." Eleanor looks over at Ameera, Lydia and Joanna. "Ach, I can just hear Joanna telling Lydia that her wee sister Ada's not doing so well. Such a shame. And her with the little ones not even at big school yet." Eleanor pauses to take a drink and eye me up. "Have you met Joanna's sister? Or heard about her?"

I've swallowed by now, so try to answer, "No, I don't bel..."

"Wonderful woman," Eleanor cuts across me, "Such a shame she's not here tonight. Her story is terrifying! You would sleep with the light on for a week after a Gathering with her in it! So, you've never heard about what happened to her at the Asylum?" Eleanor's eyes shine with excitement as she speaks.

I shake my head and keep eating. I realise Eleanor is looking for someone to talk *at*, not talk *with*, so I may as well eat my chilli while it's hot

"Well, you are in for a treat!" Eleanor says, before steering me further away from the others.

"I'm going to go out on a limb and assume that the Asylum turned out to be haunted?" I venture, between bites.

Eleanor grins wolfishly; eyes wide. "Even better!" she announces triumphantly. "One of the patients was *possessed*!"

Ah for fuck's sake! Seriously? Possession now too? I'm not sure how much more of this shite I can take. I pause eating and raise an eyebrow at her. "Really? The patient wasn't just... crazy?" I ask, trying and failing to keep the sarcasm out of my voice.

"Uh Uh. Oh no. And as Ada is a psychiatrist, she knew the difference. I know, another bloody healthcare professional. We're drowning in them around here. Anyway, after her second maternity leave, she took a role at an insane asylum in Leenane, Connemara. Do you know it? It's a beautiful part of Ireland with the fjord and the mountains."

"I know you're not supposed to say 'insane asylum' anymore, but you know what I mean. A nut house! And an old rundown one at that. It was built in the 1800s and its official title was Leenaun House, spelt the old Irish way, but all the locals just call it the Asylum. Being in such a stunning place, they'd no end of people wanting to send their ill relatives there for treatment, but they couldn't staff the place for love nor money. As the job came with paid accommodation, albeit a rundown cottage on the grounds, Ada decided to take it for a few years to save a deposit for a house."

Eleanor pauses for a sip of wine and looks furtively over her shoulder, checking to see if we are being overhead. We aren't. She continues in a lower tone. "Poor Ada would have no luck at all if she didn't have bad luck. God love her. Did you hear about her marriage? Her husband left her while she was pregnant with their second child. He shagged a bridesmaid at a wedding they'd attended together, if you can believe it! Going at it with a bridesmaid while pregnant Ada was asleep in their hotel room with their young daughter. Then he announced he'd never really loved her, ditched her for the skanky bridesmaid, never saw his daughter again, and never even met the baby! Bastard. It was the talk of the place. And she was such a beauty with her long auburn hair. She and Joanna don't look alike at all.

Anyhoo, that's how she ended up with two young kids in the arsehole of Ireland, starting a job no one else wanted. Because even though she earned good money, being a single Mum is fucking expensive, you know? That's where this story begins."

Chapter 6

Ada's Story - 'Patient A,'

told by Eleanor.

"On her very first day at the Asylum, Dr Joyce, the old psychiatrist who was due to retire soon, hence the need for Ada, and some nurses gave her a tour of the facility. At the end of the tour, they reached a door with an honest to God crucifix on it. Through the glass window, Ada saw it open into a long corridor. It's rural Ireland, so it's not that unusual to see a cross in a hospital, but it's not typical, you know?

Ada went to open the door, but Dr Joyce stopped her. He said there was only one patient in that corridor, a woman who'd been there for years, known as 'Patient A.'

Patient A, Dr Joyce explained, never left her room and no longer received any medical treatment. Ada thought they were winding her up, as you would. But no, Dr Joyce and the nurses were serious. They told her that not only was it forbidden to enter the corridor or see the patient, but they also kept all the rooms on the entire corridor free of other patients.

"Whatever for?" asked an incredulous Ada. With eight rooms in the corridor, they could have accommodated seven more patients. The facility had a long waiting list, so it didn't make any sense.

Dr Joyce said he knew what he was about to tell her would be hard to accept, but they were in no doubt that the patient was possessed. They had long turned away from medicine and towards the church to help her over the years, but all exorcism attempts had failed. All they could do was to keep her locked up and check on her regularly, but only with a priest present. They'd stopped allowing other patients to be in close proximity to her, as everyone close to her complained of terrifying experiences and inevitably deteriorated in health. This was also why the staff limited their time with her. Her food and water were always delivered by two orderlies, so they could watch each other for signs of being affected by her.

Ada laughed out loud then, convinced they were joking. But they were completely serious. They led her away and continued with her induction.

At the end of her first day, Dr Joyce gave her Patient A's file notes for her to read under supervision, in case she tried to take any photos or smuggle out some pages. He said he knew she would struggle to believe what she was being told, but begged her to trust him and never, ever enter the corridor to try to see or treat the patient alone. Ada noticed Dr Joyce looked old and haggard beyond his years. She wondered if he'd been affected by being around the patients for too long in that gloomy and desolate place. She solemnly swore to Dr Joyce that she wouldn't try to see the patient. But really, she was already wondering how she could get the poor woman out of there and get her some help.

Later that day, she read the file and, just like Dr Joyce had said, it was full of reports on failed medical treatments and interventions, as well as detailed write-ups on the many failed exorcisms. She couldn't believe what she was reading! She hadn't expected the Asylum to be as modern as newer facilities in Dublin, Cork or Belfast, but treating a patient for possession? This beggared belief.

After her kids were in bed, Ada rang a trusted colleague from her old job and told her everything over a glass of wine. The colleague had heard of patients being treated for possession in years gone by, maybe up to as recently as the sixties, but was gobsmacked to hear it was still happening. They agreed the woman needed to be rescued and formulated a plan. For this to work, Ada would need concrete evidence.

From then on, Ada often tried to get in to see the woman on her own but the other staff, of all levels, seemed to be shadowing her everywhere she went. It was like an unwritten rule. Even the cleaners kept an eye on her. She was given access to everywhere except that lonely corridor where the poor woman languished alone.

Ada became obsessed. She read and reread the woman's file. She tried to ask questions but only received curt, one-word answers. In the evenings, she googled possessions and exorcisms and became more and more convinced it was how the church categorised and 'treated' poorly educated, mentally unwell parishioners such as schizophrenics and the like, in the past.

Eventually, after a few frustrating weeks of not making any headway, who shows up? The priest! Turned out he came on the last Friday of the month to allow them to clean the room and physically check the patient over. Dr Joyce said they'd discussed it and agreed it was time for Ada to meet the patient. He handed her a gold crucifix, saying it had been specially blessed in Rome, and instructed her to wear it over her heart.

Well, Ada was so pissed off by all the bullshit at this point, she put the necklace on and tucked it under her shirt in front of Dr Joyce and the nurses, then took it off and slipped it into her desk drawer when they weren't looking. What kind of an idiot did they take her for?

The Priest, Ada, old Dr Joyce and two burly orderlies, one male, one female, prepped for the visit. Dr Joyce warned Ada that Patient A might try to connect with or manipulate her somehow. He said she must stay strong and not interact with her at all. If Ada felt Patient A trying to communicate with her, she must tell them immediately. No matter what form it took.

Ada solemnly promised she would, worried they wouldn't let her join the visit if she showed her disbelief too much. In reality, she was planning to secretly photograph and film as much as she could on her phone as evidence for staging an intervention with the help of her old colleague. The Priest unlocked the door to the corridor and led the party past the empty rooms towards the ward at the end. It was freezing. And not just 'the heat's been off for too long' cold. Really cold.

As they proceeded, Ada heard soft singing coming from the bottom room.

'Down by the apple tree, that is where I'll be.'

Ada frowned; she thought she recognised the voice and the words to the song but couldn't quite place it. It was a wistful, folksy song about lost love.

The singing grew louder as they moved closer to the room at the end of the corridor. Then the smell hit her, human shit. Lots of it. She started to gag.

"Brace yourselves," said the male orderly.

“Has everyone got their crucifix in place?” asked the priest. Ada nodded, patting her chest where the crucifix should have been, just as the others did.

“It’s awfully quiet,” said the female orderly. “It’s normally swearing at us by now.”

She isn’t an ‘it’, thought Ada in frustration. And *she* wasn’t quiet at all as the singing kicked up a notch.

‘Down by the apple tree, that’s where I’ll wait for thee.’

Again, she tried in vain to place the voice and the song. It was like trying to remember a dream.

“You’re not up to anything, are ye, Miss?” the female orderly asked her harshly.

Shocked at her insolence, Ada shook her head and curtly assured her that she wasn’t.

“Come on,” said Dr Joyce “sooner we get started, sooner we can get out again.”

The Priest cautiously unlocked the door before leading the way, followed by Dr Joyce and the two orderlies. Ada entered last and recoiled in shock. She said it was like being transported through time to another era entirely; a scene from a Victorian madhouse. There was shit everywhere, all over the floors and walls. The stench was indescribable. It looked like it may have been writing or symbols originally but was so smeared and thick that it was impossible to tell. On the bed was a hunched bag of bones, barely clad in an open robe. Filthy, matted hair was pulled forward over the woman's face. Her body was withered, wasted, and covered in sores.

Ada was *horrified*. How could they let someone live like this? The singing continued to grow in volume, surprisingly strong from the tiny-framed wretch on the bed.

'Down by the apple tree, that's where they found me.'

Could no one else hear that? Ada wondered. And where on earth had she heard that song before? At last, with a jolt of horror, she remembered.

Shortly before they moved to Leenane, she had heard the song at her daughter's school play in Belfast. The children were learning about World War II. The schoolgirls were playing the parts of land girls, singing and pining for the soldiers. That's where she'd heard the song! At the school musical.

But the school kids had written the song. The teacher announced it at the end of the play and all the parents applauded them for it.

It wasn't an actual old song. So how the hell did this isolated woman know the lyrics?

It dawned on Ada then that something was really wrong here. The singing stopped, replaced by a light chuckling laughter. With growing terror, Ada watched as the female orderly lifted the woman's matted hair and started to clean her face.

Ada's whole world turned sideways. Instead of an old woman's face, Ada saw her daughter's face, looking right at her with milky white eyes. The woman/daughter smiled at her then, a grotesque rictus grin showing rotted black teeth.

"Do you like my song, Mummy?" It asked, in a demonic voice, all trace of humanity long gone.

Ada screamed.

"I fucking knew it!" Shouted the female orderly. "Get her out of here, now!"

The male orderly grabbed Ada by the wrist and yanked her into the corridor. He pulled the neck of her shirt back and groped for the crucifix chain.

"I didn't wear it." Ada said, hopelessly. She could hear the priest shouting prayers in the room.

"Jesus! You stupid bitch!" Shouted the stricken orderly. "What have you done?"

"Just go!" Dr Joyce came out and shouted at her, pushing her down the corridor. "GO!"

Ada just about managed to get back to the corridor door; legs like jelly. Other team members who were on standby saw her coming and rushed to meet her, helping her to a seat. She couldn't stop shaking and crying.

As she told them through tears what had happened, they asked where she'd put her crucifix and went and fetched it for her. But as they fastened it around her neck, she could tell by their faces they thought it was too little, too late. Ada tried to leave. She was too scared to stay in that place any longer and fearful for her daughter. But the staff wouldn't let her go until she spoke to the priest, and she was too afraid to argue.

Later, Ada was questioned by the priest and Dr Joyce on what she'd seen and heard. She was open and told them the truth. Neither of them seemed surprised. She expected them to be angry with her but they both just looked worried, which was worse.

"What is that thing?" Ada asked.

"I haven't been able to name it definitively," said the Priest wearily, "but it's demonic. There's no doubt about that."

The priest gave her a list of prayers and instructions on how many times to repeat them and said he would call to see her the next day with more instructions. He would seek advice from the church on what to do next.

Ada nodded and thanked him.

Then, she went to the cottage, threw as much of her stuff into her car as possible, went to the kids' new school, yanked them out of class and drove back to Belfast at a hundred miles an hour. They all moved back into her parent's house. Dr Joyce and the priest tried to contact her many times, but she refused to speak to them."

Chapter 7

The Gathering, 20:05

Eleanor wipes at her eyes, clearly upset.

"That was about a year and a half ago. And about six months after she returned, she became ill. It's been just awful. As I said, some people would have no luck at all if they didn't have bad luck. Thanks for listening. It's great to get some new blood at these evenings. And the others will behave better in front of someone they don't know well. It makes me so mad that we barely even acknowledge that poor Ada can't join us anymore, and her story goes untold. So, thanks. I appreciate you listening."

"Listening to what?" Joanna asks sharply, having just materialised in front of us.

Eleanor and I lock eyes, unsure what to say.

"I was just telling your, uh, your woman here about Ada's experience in Connemara." Eleanor admits sheepishly.

"Oh? Did I not text you earlier and say I'd prefer if we didn't discuss Ada tonight? Or was that to a different WhatsApp group?" Joanna says icily.

Oh Lord! I hold my breath, wishing the floor would swallow me up.

"Uh no. You did text that, Joanna. It's just such a good story, I didn't want um, her," Eleanor gestures to me with her wine glass, "to miss out on it. We are here to tell scary stories, aren't we?" Eleanor answers in a stronger tone, trying not to be too cowed by her friend.

"Evidently." Joanna answers waspishly before giving us a thin-lipped smile and walking off to join the others.

I exhale, noting my elevated heart rate. "Um, thanks Eleanor. It was a good story. I appreciate you telling it to me. Do you mind me asking? What is wrong with Ada?"

"Has Joanna not told you?"

"No. I just know that she's ill."

Eleanor looks around before answering. "Well, you heard Joanna. She doesn't want us discussing her tonight. Maybe she has her reasons for keeping her illness private." And with that, Eleanor pats my arm before returning to the dining table, still dabbing at her eyes.

Holy Moly, what a story! Surely it isn't true. It must be an excuse for not sticking with a shit job in the arsehole of nowhere. Or maybe Ada just felt pressured to contribute at one of Joanna's bloody 'Gatherings.' At least I know now why I'm here; new listeners are needed to keep things interesting and keep the peace. I guess you could hardly put up a Facebook post asking for volunteers. Sarah and LA are still pointedly eating at the table, not joining the rest of us around the breakfast bar. When they finish eating they bring their dishes over and huffily help load the dishwasher.

"Okay everyone, you should be a lot fuller and hopefully a little less tipsy by now." Joanna says loudly, capturing everyone's attention again. "We've more tales to tell. Can you all make your way back to the table?" She claps her hands to let us know she's serious. We all shuffle back obediently, filling glasses and nabbing nibbles as we go.

Once we're all seated, Joanna clears her throat. "I'd like to remind everyone," she begins, looking around the table before fixing her gaze directly at Lydia, "that this is a safe space for everyone to speak honestly, without judgement."

Lydia smiles brightly back at her, not remotely fazed by the rebuke. "Why don't I go next?"

Chapter 8

Lydia's Story – 'The Unseen Children'

~~~

Lydia: *I realise everyone here has the right to tell their stories. But that doesn't mean we have to take them at face value.*

And now bloody Sarah's in a huff. Well, what's new? She's always feeling aggrieved about something. Bloody NHS mentality, nothing's ever right. No one else ever works as hard as them. Worse than bloody teachers.

LA is almost as bad. Urgh, her ridiculous 'tale.' Hands under the pillow? I mean, really. In fairness, I wouldn't admit to poking my own eye out either.

I just think my story should have a little more, what's the word? Status? Credibility? After all, I've walked step by step with the paranormal all my life.

I've said it before, but I'll say it again. This is the last one of these bloody 'Gatherings' I'm attending.

I refused Joanna's invitation THREE times.

Good Lord, that woman is pushy. No one would dare tell her no.

Best get on with it and get this bloody night over with.
~~~

~~~

"Those of you who have known me from childhood are aware I have a long, long history of seeing and experiencing things that defy explanation. I grew up outside Belfast, in an old house in a rural hamlet called Boardmills, near Saintfield. Before it was converted into a residential home, the original building belonged to the neighbouring church. It was known as a 'Wake House.' So, the strange things that happened there were not surprising .

Wake Houses were used in times gone by to house the dead overnight before their funerals, if the body couldn't be waked in its own house. It would mainly be used for the wakes of vagrants and criminals, or anyone without family to mourn them. The house had unusually wide doors for getting the coffins in and out through a separate entrance and exit.

Superstition had it that if the spirit of a recently deceased saw its own body, the shock would stop it from being able to cross over. To prevent this, coffins were always taken in one direction through the house, from back door to front door, never crossing their own path. That way if the spirit was trailing behind, they would think they were at someone else's wake. That's also why the mirrors were covered, so a spirit couldn't see its reflection,
~~~

or the coffin in the mirror behind it. These things are easily dismissed in the daylight, but in Boardmills at night you'd have believed in the fairies themselves. And not good fairies. No, the fairies of my great-granny's childhood that stole little babies and tormented mothers into madness.

I'd hear footsteps upstairs, running from one room to the other. I'd leave a room with wardrobes, cupboards, or kitchen drawers firmly closed, only to return moments later and find them open.

Things moved and rearranged themselves when no one was looking. Like the fruit bowl being emptied, and the fruit piled under a table.

Some items would vanish altogether. These would usually be personal items like jewellery or treasured keepsakes.

Once, I felt a breath right beside my ear, making a wisp of my hair rise and fall in front of me.

The worst experience was the hooded figure, watching me from the end of the hallway. I peed in a vase that evening, rather than walk down to the toilet. And all this while I was alone in the house.

I wasn't the only family member to have experiences like this, but the adults discouraged us from discussing it. It was almost comical.

I remember, at dinner one evening, asking who had been in my room and taken my dragonfly brooch. We didn't get many gifts, and the brooch was from a much loved, older cousin. Mum nearly took the head off me! She started shouting at me, yelling that I hadn't taken care of it, and why could no one in this house look after their damn belongings. Even Dad was taken aback. He winked at me and said he was sure it'd turn up when I needed it most. As if that made any flipping sense.

I shouldn't be so hard on Mum and Dad. Acknowledging that the strange goings on were really happening would only have made it more real, which would have led to us having to do something about it.

Besides, for long periods, years even, we'd have no activity at all. The house was, well, still is, beautiful. So, even though we'd be freaked out now and then, no one wanted to leave.

Mum and Dad stayed there until just recently when Mum couldn't manage the steep stairs anymore. So, they sold up and moved into a bungalow. They said that towards the end, it was almost like the house was looking out for them. One night, Dad had a vivid dream that there was a hooded man in his room, shaking his arm. He woke up drenched in sweat, heart pounding with fear. It was unusual as Dad never had nightmares.

Unable to get back to sleep, he got up to get a glass of water in the kitchen. There, he realised the tumble dryer had malfunctioned and had been stuck tumbling towels for hours. It was so hot it was glowing and smoking. He couldn't even touch the towels to take them out. He's pretty sure he switched it off just before it caught fire. He'd have struggled getting himself and Mum out of the house in an emergency, so it's best they've moved.

I was the only one in the family who experienced other incidents outside of the house: a small hand squeezing mine during the night in a hotel room. People disappearing, seen plainly one minute and gone the next. And, of course, the incident in Joanna's house.

Mostly, I could live with it.

But nothing, and I mean nothing, has frightened me like the sleep paralysis I've experienced. If you Google sleep paralysis, you can read rational explanations for what causes it. Essentially, during REM sleep, the rapid eye movement they teach us about in Biology, our brains inhibit muscle movement, to stop us acting out our dreams. It's called REM Atonia. Sleep paralysis occurs when your mind becomes awake but your body remains temporarily paralysed due to lingering REM Atonia. This means you experience your dreams as if they're real, but you're frozen in place, unable to move.

But the reason they're so scary is, they don't feel like dreams. In the midst of one, you feel certain you're awake. But you're frozen in place, vividly feeling, seeing, hearing and feeling things around you, feeling fear and dread.

You don't have to search very hard online to find the *other* explanation of what sleep paralysis is. It says that between sleep and wakefulness, the veil between our world and the spirit world is so thin, spirits can touch the living, and the living can feel the dead.

In Irish Celtic Folklore, experiencing sleep paralysis was considered a visit from 'The Old Hag.' Visitations from said Hag were meant to signify a warning or a punishment for a misdeed. They were so named as those who experienced it said they would feel someone sitting on their bed or pressing on their chest. Upon waking, they sometimes saw a wizened old crone near to where they slept.

In the Middle East, Djinns are blamed. Africans tend to blame witches, with some cultural variations.

As you can tell, I've done my research and, for obvious reasons, I much prefer the first theory, the REM Atonia. And apparently it is medically proven beyond any doubt.

However, if you haven't experienced sleep paralysis for yourself, it is almost impossible to convey just how terrifying an experience it is. It's really no wonder people believe the Folklore.

I've had two times in my life when I experienced sleep paralysis over a period of months.

The first was when I was a teenager in my old home. Between the ages of about thirteen and sixteen, it would happen every few weeks. Every time was different, and yet exactly the same. I'd wake and lie there, unable to move. Then, I'd sense people in the room with me.

They were never nice people. They didn't want to stroke my hair or hold my hand. No, I'd feel rough hands reach through the bars of my headboard, feeling around my head with their long nails, before grabbing big fistfuls of my hair and dragging me up the bed, as if trying to drag me through the wall and out of the very house itself. I would vividly and painfully feel the bars of my headboard digging into the top of my head. I'd try to raise my arms or kick my legs, but I was completely frozen. The pressure built on my scalp until I thought my head would crack like an egg. Then I'd jolt awake, still in the same position, my head nowhere near the bars of the headboard, heart hammering, crying with fear.

Other times, I'd become aware of people beside my bed, looming over me. I'd feel the covers being taken off me; literally feel the weight of the duvet lifting up and the cold air on my skin. Then a hand on my stomach, feeling and pressing down before it would lift up and thump back down, winding me. I'd lie frozen, twitching, trying to wake myself as I was punched over and over again in the stomach.

It happened so often, in various ways, that I started to be aware that it was sleep paralysis, and I'd try my best to wake myself. The closer I'd get to wakefulness; the more panic would build. The behaviour of the others seemed to intensify, like they were trying to really hurt me before they couldn't touch me anymore. I'd be terrified that this might be the day they weren't gone when I woke.

By the time I was sixteen, I'd developed severe insomnia and kept falling asleep in class. I was on track to completely tank my GCSEs. My parents had largely dismissed my sleep paralysis up until that point, saying I'd grow out of it and that it was all part of being a teenager, but God forbid it would make me fail my exams!

Mum marched me to the GP to get sleeping pills. I was furious with her! I did not want to take anything that could make it harder to wake up. To Mum's annoyance, I demanded to see the GP on my own. I was sixteen, for Christ's sake! I took a chance on the doctor and just told her the truth. The whole truth. The sleep paralysis, sensing the people in my room, seeing things in the house, the house history - everything just came out.

To my surprise, the GP was fantastic! She didn't tell me I was seeing things or imagining things. What she advised was; get up early, really early, far earlier than I needed to, using a really loud alarm clock so it fully woke me. Exercise more, eat healthily and cut out all stimulants. I was seriously addicted to Diet Coke at the time, so that was the hardest change to make. Her advice worked. Getting up so early and exercising more meant I was properly tired in the evenings. Instead of lying awake worrying until late, I started falling asleep earlier and sleeping soundly before being woken fully by my blaring alarm clock at the crack of dawn. Fairly quickly, the sleep paralysis stopped. I aced my exams and pretty much forgot about it. Once I hit my twenties and moved out of the Wake House, the unexplained experiences stopped too.

The sleep paralysis came back with a bang when I was in my thirties and pregnant. I think the change in hormones must have triggered it. Maybe that's why it was so bad in my teens too.

David and I always wanted kids and had only been married about five months when I got my first double lines on the pregnancy test. We were delighted! I wasn't even sick in the first few months. The only downside was the unexpected side effects of pregnancy tiredness. I was shattered all the time. I'd struggle to stay awake past 9pm but wouldn't sleep through the night. That's when it would happen.

At three or four in the morning, the sleep paralysis came back. It was just as terrifying as I remembered it. Figures by the bed. Rough hands on me. Being scratched, punched and clawed at. I'd lie there terrified, heart pounding with fear, willing myself to wake up. I was honest and told David the whole history of my sleep paralysis and how it had returned. He had never experienced it himself, but thankfully, he didn't doubt it was real, or that it was really scary. I had him act as a guardian. He had to shake me awake if he noticed me twitching or making funny noises. Some chance! He slept like the fucking dead.

Then one night, without any warning, it happened a little differently. Normally, I couldn't see. That was one of the main symptoms. I'd always have my eyes closed, and I'd be lying prone, willing my body to open them. This time, I could see. I was awake, paralysed, and staring into the eyes of the grey, dead baby sitting on my stomach, staring back at me.

It was horrifying. As I lay there staring at it in terror, it started to move. Slowly, it bent forward and started to crawl up my chest. It had just reached my face, glaring at me intently with its dead, black eyes, when I jolted awake.

God, I sobbed. I'd never experienced anything so frightening. I rang in sick and lay on the sofa all day, feeling sorry for myself. I couldn't even bring myself to tell David what happened. I just said my hormones were playing up and I had pregnancy headaches. This awful, gnawing feeling of dread grew within me. I couldn't stop thinking that there was something wrong with my baby and that what I'd seen was some kind of vision. When the bleeding started, brown blood, the kind you need to worry about, I wasn't surprised. I knew before they confirmed it at the maternity ward. I knew. My baby was dead.

The sleep paralysis stopped instantly. Only to start again, right on cue, when I got pregnant for the second time a year or so later. I thought it was scary before, but the added worry that I'd see that dead baby again made it much worse. Every time I'd feel it coming on, when I'd feel awake but unable to move, real visceral panic would set in. Inevitably, I ended up becoming really unwell. My blood pressure was so high that the GP wanted me to spend time in the maternity ward for observation.

Terrified of having the paralysis in a hospital, I refused. David didn't know what to do with me. He couldn't understand why I wouldn't take the doctor's advice. So, I'd lie and pretend I was better, even though I looked like shit and woke drenched in sweat every morning.

Eventually, I saw the dead baby again. Once again, I was awake and unable to move, eyes open, lying on my side and utterly terrified as I watched the dead, grey baby looking back at me on the pillow with its black eyes. Do you know, I was almost relieved? I could finally stop dreading the worst. The brown blood came shortly after.

It was two years and a lot of expensive marriage counselling before we tried again.

This time, I was ready. I had a strategy!

First, I told my Mum what was happening. Everything. The whole truth. Mum didn't believe me, but I harangued and browbeat her into helping me nonetheless. I made her fake chronic insomnia and fatigue, so she could get some proper sleeping pills from her GP and pass them on to me. I'd go to bed at nine pm and set an alarm for midnight. Upon waking, I'd take half a sleeping pill. Five hours of dreamless sleep would follow, until my phone alarm loudly woke me at five am and I got up.

Miraculously, it worked. No sleep paralysis.

Mercifully, the twelve-week scan showed a healthy baby with a strong heart rate. Once I got to about fourteen weeks, I took the plunge and weaned myself off the sleeping pills.

Still no sleep paralysis. Success!

When Niamh was born, I worried there might be after-effects from the pills. But thanks be to God, she was a perfectly healthy wee girl. David knew some of what I was up to. He couldn't miss the midnight alarms, and he'd seen the pills by my bed. We just didn't have the words to talk about it.

The guilt was enormous. I knew I'd put our baby in danger. Who was I to judge the effect of half a sleeping tablet on a tiny embryo, week after week? But I couldn't face losing another baby like that. Women miscarry every day, as they have for centuries. Each loss is both universal and utterly personal. Mine were brutal. But there was no going back. I'd taken the risk, and it seemed to have paid off.

It wasn't a spoken decision between David and me to stop at one child; we just didn't try for another one. The last few years had taken their toll on both of us. We didn't want to push our luck.

If ever I thought back to those early pregnancies, I only remembered the dead babies in my bedroom. My rational brain told me, in a prim and sensible tone, that it was my body's way of communicating to me in my sleep that my baby had already died, to allow me to prepare for what followed. My irrational brain would maliciously whisper that the spirit of my dead children had been trying to communicate with me, furious with me for letting them die.

No wonder I tried not to think of them very often, eh?

Niamh was a cracking wee toddler. A whirling dervish of boundless, reckless energy. One minute, she would be funny and affectionate, and the next, devious and demanding. She could be a right wee witch as well, when she wanted to be. She knew how to push my buttons. I took her outside as much as possible, trying in vain to tire her out and stop her trashing the house or giving me backchat.

When she was about four, we were sitting on a bench eating sandwiches in Ormeau Park, Belfast's largest city park and our second home, when a strange woman came and joined us on the bench. She was mid-thirties, dressed like she'd raided a charity shop, in cheap, mismatched clothes and battered DMs, with badly dyed blue hair. She looked like a grown up, homeless druggie, Coraline.

The woman gave me a wide, mad smile then said matter-of-factly, in a high-pitched girly tone, as if asking for directions to the nearest bus stop, "Are you aware there are two dead children standing behind you?"

I stopped, stock still, and stared at her. My mouth dried and my heart quickened. While I tried to form a response, Niamh chimed in. "Oh, them? They're almost always there. Mummy just ignores them."

I turned to stare wide-eyed at Niamh while she contentedly bit into her sandwich.

"Oh, I see! I knew it." The stranger singsonged happily, looking at Niamh as if she'd just been given great news. "Anytime I see The Others, it's always with someone else who sees them too." She looked at me again, with a large, stupid grin. "I just assumed it was you!"

"Get the fuck away from us." I snapped at her.

The woman stopped smiling.

"Mummy! That's Daddy's special football word! You can't say it if you're not watching a football match!" Niamh admonished me, as she spun round in her seat to face towards a wall a short distance behind us. "The lady's only asking about them 'cause they're standing right there." Niamh pointed to the wall.

My stomach lurched and my heart started racing. I forced myself to look at the wall. Shadows the shape of two small children fell on the grass and the stone wall. I looked around desperately, trying to see what trees could be casting the shadows. There weren't any.

"Can't ya see them too, Love?" The woman's voice was low and gravelly now.

"I said get the fuck away from us." I hissed at her, frightened now.

Obliviously, Niamh piped up again. "Yeah Mummy, why can't you see them too? They're always looking at you. They never look at me."

The woman moved closer towards us on the bench, making me recoil back. She looked hard, bitter, and world-weary. "Yeah Love, they're looking at you. They must want something. Or want to know something. Like, what did ya' do to them?"

"Shut the FUCK UP! And get away from us!" I yelled at her, not caring who heard.

"Mummy!!" Niamh swung back around, and I pulled her roughly on to my knee, wrapping my arms tightly around her. I glanced at the wall again. The shadows on the wall had moved; they were further to the ground and longer on the grass. They were moving closer to us. Panic started to build.

"Did ya not want them, huh Love?" The woman loomed over me threateningly. I could smell stale cigarettes and pot on her breath.

"LEAVE US ALONE!" I roared. Niamh shrank into my arms, flinging her hands over her eyes.

"Not suit ya, being pregnant, HUH? Two wee problems to be got rid of?"

"I SAID LEAVE US ALONE! NOW!" I was really panicking now.

"Coupla' wee trips to Liverpool, was it? Get them scooped out before your granny had to be told the bad news, eh? That you were a wee hoor?"

"Why would you go to Liverpool?" asked Niamh, arms still over her face.

I looked toward the wall again. The shadows were only on the grass now, the base almost touching the bench. I was absolutely terrified.

"D'ya want *me* to tell her why Belfast mummies go to Liverpool?" The woman whispered maliciously, clearly enjoying herself.

That did it. Time stopped, and my heart slowed. A roaring whooshing sound filled my ears, and everything around me faded away.

I *threw* Niamh off my knee, through the air onto the concrete path.

Then, I flew at the woman across the bench.

"I DIDN'T ABORT MY BABIES, YOU STUPID FUCKING BITCH!!" I bellowed while raining blows down on her.

Honestly, from that point on it was such a blur. I'll have to give you the witness reports from the many, many people in the park who were later questioned by the PSNI.

According to them, out of nowhere, I attacked a woman by pulling her down onto the concrete path and punching her over and over again on her face and head, while screaming "SHUT THE FUCK UP" at the top of my lungs. The woman had her arms up, trying to defend herself, shouting for help while I rained blows down on her like a woman possessed. Niamh stood howling beside us until, mercifully, a couple of capable cyclists rushed over and pulled me off the woman.

But I couldn't be calmed. All the pent-up grief and rage came bursting out of me. I roared blue murder at the woman, and it took both cyclists to hold me back. The woman and Niamh were still crying on the path when the police arrived.

Well, I soon calmed down in the police cell, I can tell you.

Breathalysed then locked up like a common criminal waiting to be questioned, I couldn't make sense of what happened. Not of what the woman or

Niamh had said, or of how badly I'd reacted. I was never violent! I hadn't thrown a punch in my life before that day. Had I really seen the shadows? Was that what upset me? Were my dead children really following me around? How could I not have noticed them before? I barely spoke during the police interview and just claimed I couldn't remember what had happened or why I hit the woman, just that she'd been harassing us. The solicitor that David called managed to get me released, promising I'd come back to make another statement after I'd been to the GP for assessment.

The police were mightily unimpressed, at first, until they identified the woman. It transpired she had quite a history of 'upsetting' strangers. A number of official complaints had been made over the years She had restraining orders filed against her from a few individuals too. They wouldn't tell me what they were about, but I could guess. She also had a history of alcoholism and drug abuse and was a petty thief, which obviously helped.

After a few months, the Public Prosecution Service advised that the assault charges against me should be dropped. Praise Jesus! However, as the assault had taken place in front of Niamh, we'd been assigned a social worker to check that she lived in a safe environment.

Christ, it was embarrassing. Whenever they pulled up outside the house, I imagined all the neighbours knew who they were.

I told David the truth. Well, most of the truth. I told him what the woman had said but didn't mention the shadows. He was pretty stoic about it. I mean, what could he say really?

Waves of shame kept washing over me. I'd assaulted a perfect stranger in the middle of Belfast's biggest park in broad daylight! Thank goodness I hadn't hurt her too badly, and the newspapers didn't pick up the story.

I couldn't stop thinking about the two small shadows. I looked and looked for them, but there was nothing there. I rarely left the house and ghosted my friends. But like all these things, with time, it just fizzled away and became a bad memory.

A year later, we were having a major kitchen renovation and, as we had no running water, we had to move into the Wake House for a few nights with my parents. This was shortly before they moved out for good, so we were helping them to pack up and throw things out.

It was Niamh who found the keepsakes.

While we were packing, she was playing dress up in a spare room, trying on ancient clothes that Mum had kept over the years. All the small things we'd lost were in the pocket of a seventies paisley jacket. Single earrings, a ring, a pink shell, my dragonfly brooch and more.

So many small treasures we never thought we'd see again. Mum and I stared at them in wonderment, laughing. It felt magical; like the house knew we were leaving and wanted to return what we'd lost before it was too late. Niamh took Mum to show Dad some of the treasures, leaving me in the room alone, holding the dragonfly brooch.

Suddenly, a ray of bright sunshine came through the window, bathing the room in light. A lovely feeling of peace came over me, followed by the prickly sensation that I wasn't alone.

I looked over to the back wall, and there they were. Clear as day, two small shadows on the wall, holding hands.

"I'm so, so sorry," I said, tearfully.

We stayed like that for a few minutes, perfectly still. Then one shadow lifted its small arm as if to wave. Heart pounding, I lifted mine too.

Then a cloud crossed the sun and the light faded, taking the shadows with it."

Chapter 9

The Gathering, 20:40

There isn't a dry eye at the table. Lydia takes a deep breath and smiles at everyone. Eleanor and Sarah reach out to squeeze her hand.

"I couldn't quite get over it though." Lydia continues. "I'd get angry for no reason and cry at inappropriate times, like in the fruit and veg section at Tesco when I was trying to pick a ripe mango. Things eventually reached breaking point when David threatened to take Niamh and apply for sole custody unless I got help. I was furious at the time but I realise now that he thought I was a suicide risk, and the impact of my mood swings was affecting him and Niamh a lot more than I realised. I saw a great therapist and, just like my old doctor, I told her *everything*. She was fantastic. Her advice was not to bottle things up. Keeping it all to myself was making everything worse. She recommended confiding in friends and told me that people might not be as sceptical as I feared. Of course, not everyone is lucky enough to have friends who will believe them. But then not everyone went through what we went through, eh Jo? Ameera?"

Joanna, Ameera and Lydia all nod knowingly at each other.

Lydia stands up, "I need a quick breather after that. Will we take five, Jo?"

Joanna jumps up with her trademark enthusiasm, "Of course, good idea, everyone. Get a smoke, go for a wee, get more wine, whatever you need! Back in ten!" She starts clearing plates, and I briefly wonder if I should help her. I am her cleaner after all. But screw it, I am a guest here tonight. Lydia goes outside for what I imagine is a smoke. Ameera heads to the downstairs loo. Sarah and LA sit and chat a bit longer, so I linger with them.

"Didn't hurt any that her David's a police officer!" Sarah says, bitchily to LA and me.

"Or that her auntie works in social services," agrees LA while they make knowing eyes at each other. Eleanor helps Joanna clear up and refills everyone's glasses.

"Here Joanna, what about that local writer who wanted to come and join us for one of these evenings to hear the tales? I think she's after inspiration for a new book." Eleanor asks as she clears up.

"Um, yes, I saw your text about her but I thought we had enough people coming round tonight. Maybe another time." Joanna answers, head in the dishwasher.

"Yeah." Sarah adds. "We've enough going on for one night."

"Aye, you said that in your text. Why, what's going on tonight? Sure, we're all just sitting chatting. I felt terrible telling her she couldn't come after mentioning it to her. I liked her last novel. You know, the folk horror set in rural Ireland." Eleanor pouts.

"Sounds good. What was it about?" LA asks, slurring slightly.

"Ah, don't you remember? I lent it to you last year, but I don't think you ever read it. It was about the woman who saw a banshee type figure. Everyone the banshee pointed to died soon after. When the woman sees the banshee pointing to her child, she has to try and break the curse. That was the bulk of the novel, her trying to figure out how to save her wee'un, going to see mediums and seers and the like. It was good, if a little hokey." Eleanor explains, while wiping the countertop.

"I have literally no memory of this." LA says, swigging more wine. "What was it called again?"

"Jeez now you're asking. What was it again? Sarah! Can you mind what it was called? You were the one who told me about it." Eleanor asks, coming back over to the table.

"The book about the pointing banshee, spirit thing? It had one of those pretentious horror titles.

The 'insert-random-scary-word here' type of titles that sound cool but don't really mean anything. The F something or other." Sarah answers thoughtfully.

"THE FINGERING!" LA blurts.

I spit out my wine as LA and Eleanor burst out laughing.

"It wasn't 'The Fingering' ya dirty bitch!" Eleanor laughs. "The Forsaken? The Foresight? The Foreshadowing?"

"The Fusty Foreskin?" LA quips, clearly on a roll.

I laugh with Eleanor and LA, as Joanna looks on in mock horror, hands on hips. "How much wine has she had, Sarah?" she barks at the table.

"That's not even a horror title!" Sarah replies, laughing.

"Well you've clearly not had to defend yourself against a fusty foreskin in the dark." LA answers, laughing loudly.

"Harry Potter and the Fusty Foreskin in the Forbidden Forest could work as a title, I guess." Eleanor adds, egging LA on. The two women roar at their own jokes while I try to smother my giggles.

"That's it. No more wine for you!" Sarah admonishes, attempting to pull LA's glass towards her.

LA is having none of it. A very middle-class, polite wrestle ensues. LA and Eleanor continue to laugh and carry on, while Joanna and Sarah both look pissed off, frankly. What is up with those two? You'd think they don't want to be here.

While the commotion continues around me, I realise two things. One, I am desperate for a wee, and two, I, along with everyone else, am pretty drunk.

As the downstairs toilet is in use, I weave my way down the hall and up the stairs to the main bathroom. It is freezing. It hasn't even felt this cold outside. At the top, I pause to steady myself, head spinning. I will have to tell Joanna I'm calling it a night. It's almost nine pm anyway. I'm sure she'll understand.

A low growl comes rumbling out of one of the rooms. The growl is deep and throaty, as if from something big.

Fear rushes through me. It sounds like a warning. What the hell is it? The first floor is eerily quiet, no noise from the kitchen can be heard. I look towards the bedroom door where I think the noise came from, straining to see through the crack of the door. I cock my head and wait to see if I hear the growl again, heart racing.

"Aah!" I scream, as a hand grips my forearm.

"Hey You!" It's Joanna.

"Oh, thank God, Joanna. I just heard an awful noise coming from one of the rooms, it sounded like an animal."

"Ooh, one of the toy dinosaurs, no doubt. The kids got some new ones recently." Joanna keeps hold of my arm and steers me firmly back down the stairs with her. "I'm trying to keep everyone downstairs this evening. Less clearing up, you know?" She shouts over her shoulder.

As I'm manhandled down the stairs I look quickly back to the bedroom. The door is closed now. Wasn't it open? How drunk am I? I try not to fall down the stairs as Joanna awkwardly, but determinedly, pulls me down behind her. When we reach the hall, I wrench my arm back, feeling annoyed. We face each other. There's a tight smile on Joanna's face. I notice she's sweating slightly.

"It didn't sound like a toy dinosaur, Joanna." I say.

She leans towards me, and I fight the urge to lean back. "Well, I can't think what else it could be, M. Can you?" With that, she turns on her heel and clips quickly back to the kitchen.

My name is not 'M'! I say to myself, ever the coward. I stand for a few moments, looking back up the stairs, straining to hear something. Nothing.

But there's a strangeness to the silence. As I stare up the stairs to the darkened landing, I get the uncomfortable sense that something is staring back at me.

I shake myself. These bloody stories must be getting to me. I make my way back to the kitchen, thankfully feeling more sober than before. I use the now free downstairs toilet and rehearse what I'll say to Joanna about needing to head home. But when I re-enter the kitchen, the women are already reseated round the table.

"Come on, come on. Eleanor's up next." Bosses Sarah, like I'm one of her patients being called from the waiting room.

I've missed my opportunity. I pour a glass of water and take my seat between Ameera and Joanna again.

Eleanor clears her throat.

Chapter 10

Eleanor's Story – 'The Grey'

~~~

Eleanor: *What the hell has crawled up Joanna's ass? She's being a stone-cold bitch tonight. Who does she think she is? When did hosting an event give you the right to give your guests a list of what they can and can't talk about. As if we're a bunch of bloody teenagers.*

I know we need to be supportive of her while her sister is so unwell, but that doesn't give her the right to dictate everything.

Thankfully, I like retelling my story. It helps cement the events in my mind as something that really happened.

It was the worst time of my life and has shaped my thoughts ever since. I still hate being home alone, preferring to mooch around cafés and shopping centres when no one else is at home.

I'm sure the poor cleaner doesn't know what's hit her. So typical of bossy boots Joanna to assume everyone would enjoy a night of these tales, just because we like them.

They are not for the faint of heart.

~~~

"My story takes place back in the nineties when I was fourteen years old.

Mum, Dad, my older sister, Annie, and I lived in a three storey, red brick townhouse in South Belfast. We were just a boring, run of the mill, family of four. Mum and Dad were decent parents, if a little cold and distant. They both worked full-time, often working long hours.

Dad was a respected solicitor and a keen rower with the Belfast Boat Club. This was a popular boat club on the River Lagan, boasting tennis courts, squash courts and a gym, as well as the Boat House. Dad served on the Club's committee as well as being on a couple of Boards for local charities. Between rowing, squash, tennis, work events and Board meetings, he could be out almost every night of the week.

Mum worked as an office manager, had her church activities and socialised with her friends a lot. She was also a member of the Boat Club, though she only played tennis there.

For years, it was mostly just Annie and me at home. Annie 'babysitting' me was actually her, locked in her room, blasting Blondie and Alanis Morissette. There are four years between Annie and me, and at that awkward age it made a difference. I was in Fourth Year at school doing my GCSEs, and a total geek. Annie was eighteen, in Upper Sixth, effortlessly cool, on the pill and out drinking most weekends with her friends and her boyfriend.

I didn't love being home alone though. Our house didn't have the same cosy, welcoming feeling I noticed in other people's houses. It was often cold, as Mum and Dad didn't feel the need to put the heat on if they weren't home, telling me to wear a fleece and make a hot water bottle if I needed it. As they were out for dinner so often, there wasn't a lot of food in the kitchen either. Apparently, that was what my pocket money was for. It wasn't a comfortable house and I often felt uneasy and on edge when I was home alone. I always had the TV and radio on to combat the oppressive silence.

Thank goodness for my school friends. Joanna, Lydia, Ameera, Sarah and LA and I practically lived in each other's houses or spent hours on the phone. Their mums never mentioned my home life directly, but there was always an extra plate at dinner time for me at their houses and leftovers to take home. Being a slightly neglected child of middle-class, working parents is a hard circle for people to square.

At weekends, the six of us spent our days mooching round shopping centres, in the Body Shop for smelly products and Topshop for Moto jeans and sparkly tops. I wasn't allowed to stay out late, so most nights I'd be home alone. As I was the youngest in the family, my bedroom was on the second floor, up a whopping thirty-nine steps, spread over four twisty flights of stairs. The layout of the stairs features heavily later in this tale, so forgive me for taking the time to detail it. There was a long flight of stairs up to a landing, which had a separate toilet and bathroom, a short flight of stairs to the first floor where two bedrooms were. Then, two shortish flights both the same length led up to my floor at the top of the house, where my room and the spare room were.

Mum, Dad and Annie slept on the first floor where they enjoyed tall, airy rooms with the original large wooden sash windows. The second floor had been designed for servants. I had a miniscule skylight and would bang my head sitting up in bed if I wasn't careful. I didn't love being on the top floor at first, after Annie kicked me out of the bedroom we shared a few years earlier, but I soon grew to love the quiet and privacy it gave.

Mabel helped; she was our pet Rottweiler. Rotties aren't the friendliest looking dogs. People would give us a wide berth in Ormeau Park when they met her on her daily walks, but they needn't have bothered. Mabel had always been a gentle giant and, by this stage, she was getting on a bit and her arthritis bothered her. She wasn't up for chasing anyone's pet poodle round the park anymore.

Annoyingly for me, this also meant she didn't come up to visit me on the top floor as much as she used to; just once a day when she came up to spend the night curled at the bottom of my bed, farting and snoring. I'm sure it wasn't very hygienic, but it worked for both of us and Mum and Dad didn't give a shit.

Like most of those old, tall townhouses, our ground floor consisted of a long living/dining room off the entrance hall which had sofas, TV, etc, at the front near the bay window, and a small dining area that led through to the kitchen at the back of the house. From the front garden, you could look in and see right through to the back garden wall. The long galley kitchen, which was accessible from the living/dining room, was tucked behind the hall. The kitchen door was almost always open, giving it the feel of it being essentially one long room.

It was while Mabel and I were watching Countdown after school one afternoon, home alone as usual and snuggling on the sofa together for warmth, that I heard the voice for the first time.

"Get Out!" A breathy whisper, just by my ear.

I jumped out of my seat, heart pounding as I scanned the room while Mabel leapt off the sofa, barking loudly as she frantically ran in circles.

There was no one there, of course. No one could ever sneak into our house undetected. Mabel may have been getting on in years, but she was still a formidable guard dog and could hear the postman from three houses away.

I looked around to see if I could work out what had made the noise. A radio turned low? The next-door neighbours? Being in a townhouse meant we had neighbours on either side. I put my head against each wall in the living room, straining to hear. Nothing.

I nervously checked around the ground floor before returning to the sofa and calling to Mabel to calm down and climb back up beside me. She was deafening when she barked, and I worried she would annoy the neighbours if they were home.

It took me a while to put my finger on why Mabel's barking annoyed me so much. Mabel wasn't a barker by nature. We had trained her out of it, and she was more of a stealthy, defensive guard dog. Not a loud, aggressive one. But when I heard the voice, she immediately starting barking loudly and tearing round the room in circles, as if she was looking for something. While I was glad of Mabel's protection and company, her reaction meant I couldn't tell myself that I'd been mistaken or hadn't heard the voice.

We had both heard it, and it had frightened Mabel as much as it had frightened me.

The second time I heard the voice was a few weeks later when I was on my own in the tiny downstairs toilet, tucked under the stairs in the hallway.

"Get Out!" It was a distinctly female voice, louder this time, and right beside me.

I jumped off the toilet, heart racing. As I scanned the tiny room, Mabel started barking out in the hall. I rushed out, still pulling up my jeans. Mabel's hackles were up as she prowled round the downstairs, sniffing as she went.

Was someone there?

I half-heartedly looked around to reassure myself, even though I was certain I'd heard the voice in the toilet. I locked Mabel in the kitchen, grabbed my coat, and went to Joanna's house, and I didn't return until I was certain someone would be home.

I did consider telling Mum or Dad what happened, but I just knew they wouldn't believe me. They'd think I was either making it up or imagining things, neither of which would go down well. Everyone in my family was expected to be pretty self-sufficient. By that age, no one even asked if I *had* homework, let alone asked to *check* it. My homework, my responsibility. I did all the dog walking and most of the cleaning too. Tales of unexplained voices and spooked old dogs would not be tolerated.

The third time I heard the voice, things kicked up a notch. I was in the galley kitchen in my pyjamas, heating a Cadbury's hot chocolate sachet on the hob. When it came up to temperature, I turned off the gas and reached for my favourite blue and white striped cup that I had placed on the counter earlier.

SMASH!

My cup flew across the room, almost faster than I could track it by eye, and shattered against the opposite wall.

"GET OUT!" A hideous, high-pitched screech filled the room. It sounded demented.

I screamed. Mabel bounded in, barking loudly, and raced around the small kitchen. I shot through the living room and ran up to my bedroom, taking the stairs two at a time. I hid there until Mum came home and shouted at me for leaving the kitchen a mess.

It was about a month after that when I saw The Grey.

I'd avoided the kitchen for ages but, weeks passed without incident, and I couldn't keep out of it forever. I was making myself dinner with Radio 1 cranked up high. I didn't go anywhere without Mabel by then, so she was curled up in her dog's bed near my feet. The kitchen door was open into the living/dining room, so I could make a quick escape if anything happened.

As I was standing in front of the stove, stirring baked beans, movement in the living room caught my eye. It was one of Mabel's balls, rolling slowly across the floor.

I instantly understood what was happening – something was trying to lure Mabel away from me!

I looked over to Mabel who, having spied the rolling ball, was just starting to scramble out of her bed. I yelled at her to stay put, raced to the kitchen door and slammed it shut with a bang.

BANG!

Something ricocheted off the door from the other side. Terrified, I walked backwards through the kitchen, eyes fixed on the door. I bent down to pat Mabel on the head at the table. She was growling softly, her eyes also fixed on the door. I reached over and flicked off the radio, straining to hear.

Moments passed. Nothing. I stood stock still, heart pounding.

BANG!

The noise came from the closed door again, followed by softer bumps. I jumped with fright as Mabel started barking. I knew what caused the noise. Someone, or *something,* had thrown Mabel's ball at the kitchen door.

"GET OUT!" A hate-filled whisper seethed through the door.

Terrified, I moved further toward the back of the kitchen, pulling Mabel with me by the collar. From there, I could look through the wide kitchen window that overlooked the yard and see into the living room through its large picture window.

As I looked fearfully through the two windows, my heart pounding, a grey figure moved slowly but purposefully, in front of the living room window.

Oh my God! What was that? My knees buckled, and my hand flew to my face. I started to cry, my lower jaw trembling in fear.

The Grey was humanlike, but unformed. Blurry around the edges. The head shape was featureless, but I knew it was looking at me. Moments passed as we faced each other through the glass, tears streaming down my face and Mabel barking beside me. It lifted its arm and pointed it towards me. Slowly, it leaned forward and touched the window.

Suddenly, the figure appeared to cock its head to the side, before disappearing in an instant.

There one minute, vanished the next.

The living room door from the hall swung open, flooding the room with light. Annie walked in, laughing with the friends she'd brought home with her. Chatting animatedly, they threw themselves on the sofa and turned on the TV. I sank to the floor, hugging Mabel tight until I stopped crying and shaking.

By this point, I avoided ever being home alone. As my family weren't home much, this meant I had to spend a lot of time at my friends' houses or at the shops. I could have confided in my friends and turned to them for advice. I don't know why I didn't, but I just couldn't find the words to tell anyone.

I wasn't coping very well. The ever-present dread made me anxious and weepy. As I was a fourteen-year-old girl, this didn't strike anyone as too unusual. But eventually, Mum and I had a blazing row about me never being home. She was yelling at me, saying I wasn't studying enough for my GCSEs and wasn't pulling my weight about the house, as I'd stopped cleaning and walking Mabel as much. I screamed back at her that I wasn't a bloody skivvy, and she should clean her own bloody house as she was the bloody mother, not me!

Unsurprisingly, she grounded me. Unable to tell her the truth, I found myself home alone after school one day when the 'big incident' happened.

I was changing out of my uniform into jeans and tee-shirt, when the air changed. It's so hard to describe exactly; it was as if the air thinned and cooled around me. Swirling cold air caressed my bare arms. Dread flooded through me. I slowly scanned the room. The temperature continued to drop, and I watched as goosebumps formed and raised the hairs on my arms. I pulled on my clothes and went out to the landing, peering over the railing into the staircase and the floors below.

There was a clear, dizzying view from my floor right down to the entrance hall. As I peered over, I realised Mabel was barking. Shit. I hadn't heard her until I went to the landing, so I don't know how long she'd been barking for, but she sounded really agitated now, barking loudly and aggressively.

Was The Grey down there? Was I trapped?

I realised it was growing darker as well as colder, even though I could see the day was still bright through the landing window. My heartbeat quickened. I wanted to run downstairs and leave, but Mabel's barking scared me.

BANG!

The sound of a slamming door from downstairs. Was someone home?

BANG!

Another slamming door, louder this time, from the ground floor. I could identify that bang as the living room door. The previous bang must have been the kitchen or the toilet under the stairs.

BANG!

That one was the bathroom at the turn of the stairs. Nobody was home, something was trying to frighten me. It was working. I started to shake and cry, hands over my mouth, waiting to see what would happen next.

A few long moments passed before...

BANG!

BANG!

The two bedroom doors on the floor below me were flung shut hard enough to splinter the wood.

Just then, I heard Mabel start to climb the stairs. I could see glimpses of her as she quickly scaled the two flights of stairs to the first floor, barking all the while, before starting up the next two flights to my floor. Thank God! But as she reached the turn in the stairs before the fourth and final flight of stairs to my floor, I got a good look at her. And, for the first time ever, I felt afraid of her. Mabel was snarling and barking ferociously. White-eyed, drool dripping. Muzzle pulled back to show all her sharp teeth.

I watched in growing horror as she climbed the last short flight of stairs towards me.

"Mabel?"

Mabel looked positively rabid as she bounded up the last short flight to my landing, skidded a turn and, while still growling ferociously, leapt through the air towards me.

Just then...

"GET OUT!"

A deranged shout came from over my shoulder.

As I drew breath to scream, my bedroom door slammed shut behind me with an almighty CRASH, just as a forceful shove from behind lifted me off my feet and sent me flying over the banister. I felt only air around me as I tumbled over from the top floor down onto the stairs below.

BAM!

The push was so forceful, I'd spun right over and landed with a thump on my back, head pointing down the stairs, feet upwards. I was badly winded and fought to pull in shaky breaths as I frantically assessed the situation. I felt jolted and sore all over, but my right thigh emanated the kind of deep, sickening pain that indicates something is seriously wrong.

Nausea washed over me and my teeth started chattering. Fighting panic, I slowly moved my head left and right, relieved to find my neck wasn't broken. As the shock subsided slightly, I realised Mabel was still barking, if anything more ferociously than before, up on the top floor.

"GET OUT!"

That unhinged shout again, filling the house.

There was a deep thudding sound on that top stairway that sounded like a heavy footstep. I heard Mabel start making her way back down the stairs, barking frantically. Realisation hit me like a fist. It was The Grey. And, it was coming after me.

I needed to move, NOW!

I lifted my arms and placed them on the steps under my chest and began pushing myself backwards down the stairs. The pain in my leg was intense but adrenaline and fear spurred me on. I pushed down onto the first-floor landing and used my hands and remaining good leg to push myself backwards around the bend to the next short flight of stairs. Mabel's barking never ceased but I could still hear the other sound above her.

Thump. Thump. Thump.

It sounded like something was slowly stomping towards me. A primal, visceral fear came over me. I started to shake and hot tears ran down my face. I knew if I didn't keep going, I was in grave danger.

Once on the main first floor landing, I again pushed myself backwards down the short flight of stairs to the turn in the stairs. Fear threatened to overwhelm me. The pain was indescribable. Nausea came in waves. I turned my head and vomited on the carpet beside me.

I could hear Mabel had reached the stairs I'd landed on and was still coming. Her barking had slowed slightly, and I knew it was from exhaustion. She would be in need of water by now.

Thump. Thump. Thump.

Mabel was on the first-floor landing now, a short flight of stairs away from me. The last flight of stairs was too tall and steep to go down backwards, and I couldn't risk sliding down them and breaking my neck. I gathered my strength and painfully manoeuvred myself round so I was feet first, before starting the last descent.

I eased myself slowly down the stairs, trying to take my weight on my left leg, sobbing as I went. The pain in my leg was horrendous and I knew it was damaged. My whole body shook as I slid down each step, barely able to endure the pain each bump brought.

Finally, I reached the entrance hallway and stopped, panting and crying. I looked up to see Mabel barking loudly on the turn in the stairs in an attack stance. As I watched, a dark grey arm with long, cruel fingers lashed out and smacked her on the nose, scratching hard enough to draw blood.

I screamed frantically as Mabel yelped and jumped backwards, before bracing herself and leaping back to attack.

Shit. Whatever it was, it was really close now. I had to keep moving. Using my left leg and my arms, I pushed myself along the hall to the front door. I managed to twist round and open it before dragging myself out to the front garden.

Once outside, I started shouting for help. The Ravenhill Road is always busy with commuters, school kids and dog walkers. Within seconds, a man came over to help me. But as he began to push open the gate, Mabel rocketed out of the house, every inch a hellhound, blood and saliva flying from her jaws, barking ferociously as she thundered towards the man. He only just got the gate closed in time. "Fuckin' 'ell, love! Has that dog attacked you?"

For some reason, this made me laugh, even as I kept crying. The man looked really shaken up, and frankly a bit pissed off.

"No, she saved me!" I stuttered out, crying, laughing and hiccupping all at once. "Can you call an ambulance?"

"Wha? I don't have a mobile!" he replied. As I said, it was the nineties.

I lay sobbing in the yard while Mabel circled me, barking at the growing crowd gathered outside our house. Someone eventually called for an ambulance, and it arrived at the same time Annie got back from school. She arrived at the gate with the ambulance crew, face like thunder. "What the hell, Eleanor?!" she roared as she opened the gate, assuming she could come in as usual. But Mabel, who was almost deranged by this point, launched herself at her too.

"What is going on, Eleanor?!" Annie screamed again. "Right! I'll go round the back and get in that way."

Delirium was setting in, but I still had some wits about me. "Don't! There's something inside!"

Annie looked at me quizzically before making her way down the street, heading for the alley at the back of the houses from where she could get into our backyard. I waved frantically at the paramedics, who looked like they were watching a tennis match, swivelling their gaze warily from Mabel to me, then back to Mabel.

“Stop my sister, please! There’s something inside!” I yelled at them.

“What’s inside? Have ya been attacked, love? Is it another dog?” They asked, unable to make head or tail of what I was yelling at them.

“Mabel!” Annie roared from inside the house.

Mabel ran into the house. We heard the sound of a door slamming. Annie came walking out a moment later, looking shaken.

“She’s trapped in the kitchen, it’s safe.” she shouted to the paramedics.

“There’s something inside, don’t go back in. Please!” I begged as she knelt down and took my hand.

“Ssh ssh, don’t worry, it’s okay. I’ll come with you to the hospital. We’ll deal with it later.”

As they put me on the stretcher, my heart broke to hear Mabel desperately trying to escape the kitchen, scratching and headbutting the door. But everyone ignored my pleas to help her, and the ambulance took Annie and me to A&E.

The hours passed slowly at the hospital. My thigh was broken in two places. They reset it and plastered my leg from toe to thigh. Mum and Dad arrived and hung around for a while, listening with growing embarrassment to my ramblings about The

Grey in the house and how it wasn't safe for them to go home. They asked my consultant to check if I was concussed and/or crazy and had a bit of a row with him when, to their disappointment, he said I was mentally sound. It was all very awkward and a blessed relief for everyone, when Mum and Dad said their goodbyes and sloped off home with Annie. I was kept overnight for observation.

I naively thought this meant rest and monitoring, but it soon became apparent it was a ruse to allow the hospital staff to take turns quizzing me on my home life without my parents there. Did I have something I wanted to tell them? Was my Dad/boyfriend/drug dealer rough with me? Did I fall because I was high and didn't want my parents to know I took drugs? What did I mean by 'there's a Grey' in my home?

What could I say? Like LA, I buckled and backtracked nonsensically. They reluctantly discharged me the next day, though only after I'd made empty promises to 'contact someone' and 'talk when I was ready.'

Dad picked me up, grimly wheeling me down the corridors and out to the car. It had taken them all night to sort the house, apparently. They couldn't even go out! We left the wheelchair at the hospital so getting from the car to the house was an awkward shuffle.

“Where’s Mabel?” I asked when they had made me comfortable on the sofa with my leg elevated in front of me.

Mum and Dad exchanged a look. “Still at the vets.” Mum answered.

“When will she be back?” I asked.

Another look. “We’ll see.” Dad said tersely. “And we will discuss what happened, later.”

‘Later’ was when the four of us were awkwardly having dinner that evening, not a common occurrence in our house. Dad waited until we’d all been served, before interrogating me in his most patronising, courtroom tone.

“Perhaps Eleanor, you could take a few minutes to explain to us all how exactly you managed in the space of a few hours to fall over the bannisters and break a leg, vomit all over the stairs, turn our beloved pet into a snarling, rabid beast and then lie in the front garden shrieking about Grey Beings to half of Belfast at the top of your voice? Hmm? Been ‘experimenting’, have we?”

The penny dropped then. They thought I’d taken drugs, and that Mabel had accidently taken them too. Seriously? Drugs?! I didn’t even drink! I don’t think I’ve ever hated anyone so much. Mum was staring at me with a look of pious disgust.

I knew I was beaten, and they'd never believe the truth. But I couldn't get the image of that dark grey arm out of my head. And I'd had enough. We were in danger, for God's sake! I took a deep breath, and, while staring at my plate so I didn't have to watch their patronising expressions, I told them the whole story from the first "Get Out" to escaping the house yesterday. When I finished, I looked up to see Mum and Dad making eyes at each other, twisted smiles of disbelief on their faces.

"Well," started Dad, "I have certainly heard some creative excuses in my time in court..."

"I've heard the voice too. And The Grey... I've seen it too. She's not lying."

We all turned to stare in surprise at Annie. She looked pale and was even thinner than usual. I didn't know how I hadn't noticed before. Annie took a deep, shaky breath. "For me, it started about four or five years ago. A horrible female voice telling me to get out when I was home alone. But not just the voice. Sometimes it would be a slamming door, scratching sounds or things moving. Temperature changes, from warm to freezing." She paused, gathering herself. "And then I saw...something. I was looking in the hallway mirror putting on a hat when I saw something move behind me in the living room. It was hideous. A sort of human...shape. But not quite. Not a person. Not a ghost. I don't fucking know, but I got the hell out. Mabel would go mental at it." She stopped and looked at me, tears in her eyes. "That's why I go out so much. I hate being alone in this house. I always stay in my room blasting music, as I've never heard it in there. I'm so sorry Eleanor. I don't know why, but it didn't occur to me that you might hear it too."

Silence hung in the air as we all absorbed what Annie had said. I was grateful to her for saying what she did as Mum and Dad would believe her, but it was tinged with resentment as I knew they would never have believed me. And I was angry at going through everything alone when she could have warned me. Or helped me! Believe wasn't quite the right word. Mum and Dad didn't think Annie was lying, but it was a hard story to take at face value.

Stunned, that's the word. They were stunned into silence. In the end, we agreed to talk again the following night after we'd all had some rest. I worried that this meant me having to sleep on the sofa as I couldn't climb the stairs. Without Mabel, the thought terrified me.

"I'm not staying down here on my own. I mean it. I'll ring the fucking doctors and tell them I'm ready to talk if need be and go back to hospital."

They all looked at me with surprise as I was never usually this forceful.

"We'll stay with you. None of us will leave you on your own until we figure this out. Please don't worry." Annie spoke with such kindness, that a lump formed in my throat.

"Thanks Sis."

To be fair to them, they kept their word and didn't leave me on my own. Mum took a couple of weeks off work on carer's leave and sat with me all day in the living room, watching daytime TV, playing cards or reading our books. Dad and Annie spent the evenings with us, doing much the same.

One night, trying to make light of things, Dad set his digital camera beside me, joking "Maybe you can catch this Grey thing on camera, and we'll make the news." Being a solicitor, of course, he wanted proof.

The care and attention lasted about a week and a half. Then, inevitably, the burden of round the clock care for a fourteen-year-old in perfect health, aside from a broken leg, started to grate. By the end of her second week of carer's leave, Mum started popping to the shops, then popping out for coffee, then just heading to the Boat Club to hang out there and 'get her head showered.'

Mabel had come home from the vets after a couple of days, exhausted, with nasty cuts on her muzzle and stitches that annoyed her. She was allowed up to snuggle me on the sofa while we both recuperated, under my blanket with her head on my lap, while I kept my plastered leg raised. I was so grateful for what she'd done that I couldn't stop petting and kissing her. She was extra affectionate too and the days passed peacefully. The fear in my stomach abated and I even started to doubt myself.

Was I pushed? Could I have fallen, hit my head and imagined it all?

One afternoon, almost a fortnight after the fall, I was in the living room reading with the radio on. Mum and Dad were out but Annie was up in her room, supposedly taking care of me from there. Rock music started to blare from upstairs, so loud I could hardly hear my music even though my radio was beside me.

"Annie!" I shouted. Just as I realised, she wouldn't be able to hear me, the temperature in the room started to fall. Goosebumps raised on my arms. Mabel's hackles went up and she jumped off the sofa and started to prowl around the living room. My heart started to race.

"Annie!" I called again. I heard a thump on the stairs. Mabel raced out of the living room to the bottom of the stairs in the hallway and started barking. Shit.

"ANNIE!!" I roared.

Thump.

Mabel's barking went up a notch.

Thump.

I looked around in panic for my crutches. On the coffee table in front of me was the digital camera. I don't know how I managed it, but I set the camera to record and placed it back on the table, facing the door to the hallway. I grabbed my crutches and, as quick as I could manage, hopped through to the kitchen, opened the backdoor and hopped out to the backyard.

Annie's room was at the back of the house, and I looked up at her window, heart thumping. What should I do? Throw a stone at her window to get her attention? What then? I didn't want her to come out of her room in case she encountered whatever it was Mabel was barking at. A howl of pain ripped through the air.

"Mabel!" I peered through the living room window to see Mabel rolling around the living room carpet. She was locked in battle with... something. I couldn't make it out. It was black like her, but longer and more angular. Blood bloomed on the carpet beneath them. Panic overwhelmed me as I watched helplessly.

The guttural fighting noises were stomach churning. A human scream joined the melee. I looked up and could just see Annie at the entrance to the living room pulling its door closed. I guessed that after checking that I wasn't in the living room, she would run out the front door and come round to the back yard to look for me. I hopped down the yard, opened the gate, and went out to the alley. She raced down to meet me there moments later.

"Oh, thank goodness you're alright!" she exclaimed, flinging her arms around me and almost knocking me over.

I leaned on the alley wall to steady myself. "We have to help Mabel." I said, shaking and crying.

Annie was grim faced. "How?"

I cocked my head. "I can't hear her anymore."

A neighbour we were friendly with appeared at her yard door.

"Girls! What's going on? Is your Mabel in a dog fight?" she shouted.

We just looked at her with stricken faces, unable to form a response.

"Right, I'm ringing the Police. Keep you two away from them!" She shouted before she disappeared back into her yard.

Annie and I made our way slowly round from the back alleyway to our front garden and peered through our living room window. Mabel lay still in the middle of the room, a large pool of blood on the jute rug beneath her. We couldn't see any sign of what she'd been fighting with.

"I'll go and check on her," said Annie, opening the front door.

"Don't," I said, grabbing her arm. "If she's gone, she's gone. Don't risk it."

We remained outside, holding on to each other, until the police came. We didn't try to stop them from entering the house. What would we have said? They came back out to us and confirmed what we already knew. Mabel was dead. The police called our parents who came home to find us sitting sobbing beside Mabel's body, giving unsatisfactory answers to visibly sceptical police officers.

Dad took charge and soon sent the officers away to look for the 'other dog' who killed ours. Mum wrapped Mabel in the jute rug and dragged her out to the yard, where her bloodied and battered body remained overnight. Annie and I were in a daze, too shocked and saddened even to speak. Eventually, over cups of hot chocolate with a dash of Baileys, we told our parents what happened. They didn't argue with us, but it was clear they didn't believe us. I asked to go and stay with granny, but they said no, it was too late by then. Instead, Dad helped me up to the first floor where Mum, Annie and I all slept in Mum and Dad's bed while Dad slept in Annie's room. My leg ached and I slept fitfully. Images of

Mabel fighting flashed in my head, each image hitting like a sucker punch. Eventually tears came, and I cried myself to sleep.

In the morning, Dad took Mabel's body to the vet for disposal and the jute rug to the dump. Mum stayed to clean the living room. Annie and I sat out in the back yard on the wooden table and chairs, me with my leg raised. We couldn't look at the blood stain and didn't want to be in the house.

"What are we going to do?" I asked, not expecting an answer.

We could see Mum through the window, scrubbing the wooden floor on her hands and knees.

"I don't know. But we can't stay here." Annie answered flatly.

Dad came back from the vet, ashen faced. He joined us in the yard, sitting heavily on a chair beside us. "They think it was her heart that gave out in the end. She was badly injured, but it wasn't enough to kill her."

We just nodded at him.

He made a visible effort to gather himself. "Girls..." he began.

"The camera!" I exclaimed. "How did I forget? I set it to record yesterday. Check it."

Annie's eyebrows shot up.

Dad looked incredulous. "My digital camera? You filmed what happened?"

"Maybe. I haven't looked. Check it and see."

Dad went indoors, and we could see him looking for the camera while Mum took a break from cleaning to help him. The camera must have gone out of charge because Dad went upstairs before returning with the charger. Once plugged in, he and Mum sat on the sofa looking at it while Annie and I watched them through the window. Barely a minute passed before Mum screamed and Dad dropped the camera. Mum ran out to us as Dad fumbled to pick up the camera and continued to watch, open mouthed.

"What the fuck was that?" Mum shouted at us. Annie and I shrugged at her. "Answer me!" she shouted louder.

"I think it was The Grey." I said, eventually.

Mum slapped me, hard. My hand flew to my cheek.

"Mum!" Annie shouted at her.

"You're next Missy if you don't start telling me the truth!" Mum roared at her, hand raised.

Dad appeared just then and clamped his hand around her wrist. "Pack up. We're leaving."

We moved into our granny's tiny two up, two down that night and stayed until the sale of our house went through and we bought another one. We didn't talk about what happened, not properly. If we had to refer to it, we just called it 'The night Mabel died.'

Our new house was nice, further out of Belfast, with proper gardens. We didn't get another dog, even though we all missed Mabel terribly. We spent more time together and became closer as a family in our new home.

I didn't tell anyone about the night Mabel died or The Grey until I was at Uni studying Business when, why else? I was trying to impress a boy. I was drinking and smoking pot with some students from my class at a party in a grotty student rental house, hoping the best-looking guy from my class, Damian, would pay attention to me.

A student I didn't know got out a Ouija Board and, without asking, started setting it up on the coffee table. I sobered up quickly, lifted the board off the table and flung it under the sofa.

"Nope, nope, nope!" I said, arms folded on the opposite sofa, face serious.

Everyone fell about laughing at me. "Ah, come on Eleanor! It's just a bit of craic."

"No, it isn't. It's dangerous. You don't know what you're messing with. When I was younger, something I can't explain killed my dog!"

"Ah piss off! You telling us you were haunted by a dog-hating ghost?" More laughter.

After much cajoling, I ended up spilling the beans. No one believed me and who could blame them? I called it a night and staggered home so they could play Ouija without me.

At the start of an Economics lecture the next day, Damian sidled up to sit beside me. "Were you telling the truth last night?" he asked in a whisper.

Crippled with hangxiety and embarrassment, I just nodded.

"Do you still have the footage?"

I turned and raised an eyebrow at him. He flashed a megawatt smile, usually reserved for lecturers when he was trying to bluff his way through an answer he didn't know in class. "It's just, I have a dream of directing a short horror film based on Irish ghost stories and folklore. It would be great for inspiration."

Inspiration or ripping off? And a wannabe film director? Could he be any more of a cliché? In the end, I agreed to check if the footage still existed, despite not being asked on a date.

Next time I was home, I hunted through one of the junk cupboards that all houses have. To my surprise, hidden at the back in its original box, I found the camera. It hadn't been charged for years, so I plugged it in. Nothing.

Not feeling overly optimistic, I left it charging on the kitchen counter and went off to wash my clothes and raid the fridge. When I rechecked after a few hours, I found lights flashing at the top. My stomach sank as the old feelings of fear and dread came back. What was I thinking? With trembling hands, I pressed the 'on' button.

The first image on screen was of our old living room door, leading to the hallway with a triangle in the middle, inviting me to press play. My stomach lurched and I quickly scanned the kitchen, almost expecting to hear the familiar 'Get Out!'

I was suddenly very conscious I was home alone. Was The Grey really recorded on video? I knew I'd never look. I couldn't bear to see Mabel being killed. Maybe Damian would have more stomach for it. I clicked the camera off, placed it back in its box, wrapped the box in a scarf and stashed it at the bottom of my rucksack. I carried it gingerly, as if I were transporting a bomb.

At the next lecture I shared with Damian, I sat beside him. He was hungover and wearing clothes that had obviously been slept in. I handed the camera box over to him.

"Uh, thanks. What can I expect to see?" He asked, reeking of stale cigarette smoke and beer.

"Don't ask me, I haven't watched it. But I should warn you, our dog did die horribly."

"Well, er thanks again." He flashed his trademark grin, more wolfish than rakish in the harsh light of the lecture hall. "Hey, want to get a drink later? I can tell you what I saw? I'll leave out any gory details."

I hesitated, "Uh, I'm good. Sure, I'll see you in classes later this week."

Damian looked a bit pissed off. "Suit yourself." He said curtly and put the camera away.

We listened to the rest of the lecture in silence, which seems sad now as that was the last time I saw him alive.

"What did you do to poor old Damo, Eleanor?"

It was the following week, in the same class. I twisted my head to look behind me. I recognised the guy sitting behind me from some classes we shared but I didn't know his name. He was wearing the same GAA hoodie I often saw Damian in, so I guessed they were on the same team.

"Huh?"

"Damo missed practice last week and the match at the weekend. Coulda done with him. We were feckin' annihilated by Antrim."

"What's up with him?" I asked.

"You tell me. He won't say. He just asked me to ask you this, "Did you know?"

"Know what?" I asked, genuinely confused.

"You tell me."

"Or you can both tell me, after class!"

I jumped and spun around to see our Economics lecturer standing in the aisle beside me. Nervous laughter rippled round the auditorium.

"Is there something you'd like to share with us all, Eleanor?" He asked, peering over his glasses.

"Er, no. Sorry. Won't happen again." I muttered.

"How frightfully kind of you, Miss. Did you hear that class? Eleanor has agreed to be quiet for the remainder of the class. Isn't that wonderful?"

There was more laughter as the lecturer made his way back to the stage, while my cheeks burned.

I chatted briefly with the guy behind me as we were packing up our stuff at the end of the lecture. He told me he was Damian's flatmate as well as teammate, and that his name was Cathal, before rushing off to his next class.

I scanned the corridors, Student Union cafés and lecture halls for Damian every day for the next few weeks, but there was no sign of him. I tried to get Cathal's attention a few times, but he pointedly ignored me. Worry grew, until I resolved to go and find Cathal and demand an answer, so I could get Damian off my mind.

There was no need. As we filed in for our first lecture the following Monday morning, four serious looking members of staff stood on stage waiting for us. Once enough of us were seated, a lady I didn't recognise introduced herself as the 'Head of Student Welfare.'

In a sombre tone, she announced two things; firstly, that our classmate, Damian O'Toole, had died over the weekend, and secondly, we would all be offered free bereavement counselling and support.

All around me, people started to cry. Not me, snakes writhed in my stomach while I hugged a friend, who had started sobbing beside me. As I comforted her, the hairs raised on the back of my neck. I looked up to see Cathal staring at me, stony-faced, eyes burning with fury. Shit!

I managed to avoid Cathal that day, but I knew it wouldn't be so easy at the funeral.

The service was lovely. Damian's older sister gave a beautiful eulogy while his parents and younger siblings sobbed in their pew. The church was overflowing with mourners, all devastated at the loss of such a promising young man.

More details had emerged of Damian's death. He had become paranoid and delusional in the last weeks of his life, convinced that something was following him. He repeatedly called the police to his student accommodation, even though his flatmates were there and had reassured him that there was no one there. The police were pissed off and told the flatmates to get him to a doctor or he'd be arrested for wasting police time.

The doctor prescribed rest and anti-anxiety medication, but Damian's mental state rapidly deteriorated. Soon after, he had a psychiatric evaluation. He wasn't committed but had been advised to leave Belfast and go home to Cookstown to recuperate with family. He refused. His flatmates were asked to keep an eye on him.

He hadn't seemed suicidal.

They repeated that a lot.

His flatmates were awoken around three am on the night of his death by the screams coming from his room. By the time they kicked the door in, Damian had already fallen to his death from his third story window.

Fallen, or pushed?

Waves of guilt kept washing over me, making my knees weak. What if they found the camera? Apart from the video of Mabel, it must have been filled with old photos of me and my family. How would I explain Damian having it?

We were invited to the local GAA club after the funeral. I stayed close to Zoe and some other friends, and out of Cathal's way. Everyone swapped stories about Damian and there was talk of an award being set up in his name for up-and-coming players. I felt wretched. To escape the banal conversation, I made my way towards the ladies.

As I passed the disabled toilet, an arm shot out and roughly yanked me in. Once inside, Cathal locked the door, stepped towards me and calmly put his forearm over my throat, pinning me uncomfortably to the wall.

I pushed against his chest, to no avail. My heart pounded and I fought to stay calm.

Cathal took a deep, shaky breath before asking menacingly. "The fuck did you do to him, Eleanor? And don't fuckin lie to me." He pressed against my windpipe, and I pulled at his arm, trying to release the pressure.

"I, I..." I stuttered.

"Go on."

"I can't breathe. Stop, please, Cathal."

He dropped his arm and folded his arms across his chest, no longer touching me but still very much between me and the door.

"Jesus Cathal, you could've just asked me out in the club."

He blinked rapidly and I realised he was fighting back tears. My panic gave way to wary pity. I reasoned he was deep in the 'anger' stage of the grief curve the university counsellors kept banging on about, and no wiser at all as to my part in Damian's death. He just wanted answers.

I gave him a watered-down version of the story. I told him that Damian and I had been talking about a horror movie he wanted to direct, and I'd told him my sister thought she'd caught a ghost on camera, years ago. Damian had asked to see it, so I lent him our old camera the last time I saw him. I said I hadn't noticed any particularly unusual behaviour from him, other than he seemed to be drinking and smoking dope more than usual. I didn't think lending him the camera would do any harm.

Cathal listened intently. Then he told me they reckoned Damian was doing much stronger stuff than just dope and that was probably why he wouldn't go home, as he didn't have a dealer near his parents' house. The logical assumption was that the hard drugs contributed to a psychotic break and suicidal thoughts.

Something wasn't adding up, if that was true, why was Cathal so mad at me?

Cathal stared at me, po-faced. "Thing is, weeks before his untimely death, Damian burst into my room, rambling like a madman. Said he was being followed by something only he could hear. He said the same thing had happened to you, and that you'd been pushed down the stairs by something that had then killed your dog. Said ever since he'd watched a scary as fuck video on your old camera, he'd felt like something was watching him. Following him everywhere. He asked me to ask you, 'Did you know?' I, of course, asked, 'ask her did she know what?' But he didn't say anything else, and I naturally dismissed it as the ravings of a madman. However," he advanced on me again and I shrank back against the wall, "when I retold this story to a mate in the days following Damo's passing, the mate said he was at a party with you a few months ago, and that was the exact story you'd told everyone that very night."

He loomed over me; hands balled into fists by his side. "So, now I don't know what to think."

I blinked up at him, mind racing. "I, I was blocked and stoned, Cathal. I just said some shite to stop them doing the Ouija board, I hate those things. I didn't think anyone would believe me."

Cathal's jaw trembled. "The thing is, I think I heard..."

Bang! Bang! Bang!

Someone was angrily pounding the toilet door. "Far as I can see, my wee girl's the only one here in a bloody wheelchair. So, whoever is in there needs to hurry the hell up, as she can't hold it in for long."

Cathal reluctantly stepped back and opened the door. We exited sheepishly.

"Dirty bastards, it's a bloody funeral," the woman muttered, as we filed out past her. I hot-footed it away and never did hear what it was that Cathal thought he heard."

Chapter 11

The Gathering, 21:20

A shiver runs down my spine. That poor man, falling to his death. Pushed, or driven by paranoia and madness to jump.

The mood in the room is more sombre than before. No one is picking up their wine glasses. Sarah pours water for herself and those near her.

"Do you ever see Cathal around?" Ameera asks Eleanor.

"Sometimes. He lives not far from here with his wife and two wee girls. I just get curt nods from him, or a hard stare. We've never spoken since." Eleanor answers.

"Did you ever hear tell of the camera?" asks Lydia.

Eleanor gives a hard snort. "No, never. Thank God."

"Every time I hear that story, I get so mad you didn't tell us what was happening at the time. We all thought you'd just fallen down the stairs when you broke your leg," Sarah admonishes Eleanor. "I remember my Mum complaining about you being over at our house so much and asking why you never invited me over to yours. I was so self-involved, I'd hardly even noticed."

"She was probably sick of feeding me." Eleanor replies with a small smile.

"Sure, I was the same," says Lydia huffily. "I tried to tell you about the sleep paralysis and none of you believed me. And when I told you my house was haunted you stopped visiting!"

Sarah and Eleanor look sheepishly at each other.

"Well, your house was kinda creepy," says Eleanor.

"Right beside the graveyard and all," echoes Sarah, nodding.

It wasn't that we didn't believe you." Joanna says. "I'd had sleep paralysis once or twice myself and knew it could feel scary."

"Oh really, could it? Thanks for the validation, Joanna." Lydia snaps waspishly.

"Don't be huffy!" Joanna snaps back. "When things got spooky at my house, I told you about it, didn't I? See, I did believe you."

An awkward tension falls and no one speaks. I stare at my hands for a moment. Interest piqued, I turn to Joanna, "Is your story next?"

"Oh no," she answers. "I don't think we've time for mine tonight."

This is my opportunity. "Well, it is getting late..." I begin.

"Ameera, why don't you go next? Yours is only a short one." Joanna cuts over me.

Ah for God's sake!

"Short but terrifying." Lydia adds animatedly. "Hers is the only one that keeps me up at night. I was telling your story to a friend a few weeks ago and she had to sleep with the light on for a week!"

Sarah lets out a low whistle, followed by "Yep. A murderous ghost will disrupt your sleep alright."

Is sensible GP Ameera really about to tell us a tale of a murderous ghost? Maybe this is worth a listen. Resigning myself to my fate, I generously pour myself some more wine.

Ameera takes a drink of water, then pauses for such a long time that I wonder if she's going to start at all.

I look around the table. Everyone is looking sympathetically at Ameera.

"Take your time," encourages Sarah.

Ameera nods and clears her throat.

Chapter 12

Ameera's Story – 'A Hand in the Dark'

~~~

Ameera: *The poor cleaner. She's clearly not enjoying herself and wishes she could leave. I wish she would. I don't know how Joanna can be blasé about her role here tonight. I haven't been able to think of anything else for weeks.*

Not long to go now.

It'll all be over soon.

~~~

"It was the late eighties and I was about ten years old. We lived on a council estate in Glasgow, in a small, high-rise flat, far more depressing than it already sounds. The flat was a tiny two-bed with a small living room that led to a separate kitchen that could just accommodate a dining table. My mother, Priya, kept it as nice as she could, but the inherent bleakness of the building and roughness of our estate couldn't be disguised, especially on a shoestring budget.

I don't have many happy memories of living there. It wasn't just the proximity to the high death rate caused by drugs and murder on the estate, our lack of money, or my life being devoid of friends but overflowing with bullies. We weren't a happy family because of my father, Arun. And when the core is rotten, the rest of the fruit is tainted.

Arun was a lot older than Priya, well into his fifties by then, a small, greying man with hunched shoulders and a permanent scowl. He took no joy in life and was on a mission to see that those around him wouldn't either. I only remember him speaking to moan, criticise or complain. When you're younger, you take these things as a given; that all Dads are miserable gits. But by then, I was painfully aware that not everyone's Dad was an unloving, sanctimonious prick. Some were even nice to their children and their wives. Some organised cricket and football tournaments on the grass beside the high-rise and took their kids on walks and trips out. I only ever seemed to be at school or home.

I was self-aware enough to feel sorry for Priya, as well as myself. We clung to each other like life rafts in our sea of misery.

When Priya had finished school in Mumbai, she had more options than many would assume for the seventies in India. Being from a wealthy and progressive family, she had attended a prestigious university to read History and had fallen in love with a fellow student, and they made tentative plans to marry. Arranged marriages were still commonplace at that time, but not entirely ubiquitous. If two young people independently found a partner that met the expectations of their family, it wasn't unusual for the match to be met with approval.

It was her maternal grandfather who scuppered things.

While Priya was taking measured, calculated steps to secure a future with her chosen loved one, unbeknownst to her, her grandfather and his cousin were urgently scheming against her. The cousin's recently bereaved and widowed son, Arun, needed a second wife but was having trouble finding one, due to rumours of a scandal. When he announced to Priya's parents that he had found a fortuitous match for his granddaughter, Priya, the old binds and traditions held strong and couldn't be circumvented. Priya and Arun were distantly related enough for the marriage to be legal, and there was a promise of her having a better life in the UK, where they headed shortly after their wedding. I arrived about a year later.

In the brief gap between me arriving home from school and him arriving home from work, the tiny flat would briefly feel like a home. My mother and I would play board games, read books, do jigsaws or watch game shows on the tiny TV. We'd speak freely, trying to get all our words out before he came home. But it was a false, fragile good time. We'd hug too often, too tightly. We'd both check the clock too frequently, not wanting to be caught making a mess or without dinner ready. By the time my father walked through the door, the games, jigsaws and books were back in my cupboard, hidden behind some rarely worn second-hand saris.

Priya was everything to me. It was her and me against the world. I'd have done anything to rescue her.

But in the end, it wasn't me who saved her.

Our 'encounter' happened on a mundane, groundhog, mid-week summer evening. Scottish summers were almost as uncomfortable as Scottish winters. The heat rose in the building to our eighth floor flat and no one had air conditioning back then. We'd just open the tiny windows and switch on a tabletop fan to blow the hot air around. We were sitting at our small dining table, Priya and Arun at one side, and me at the other, eating our plain, homemade fare of rice, daal and chapatis in silence, listening to the whine of the fan. The ever-present frosty atmosphere stifled all conversation.

But it didn't stop Priya from communicating with me. She smiled across the table. A warrior's smile, devoid of mirth and full of strength. 'Keep your chin up', the smile conveyed, 'We'll get through this together.' Checking Arun wasn't looking, I nodded to her resolutely in acknowledgement. We were survivors. We could do this together.

That evening as we ate, Priya was worrying about me, as usual. There were dark circles under my eyes, and she'd heard me crying in my room the previous night. When she checked in on me, I'd feigned sleep, trying not to worry her. She was also mentally running through what was left in the kitchen cupboards, calculating if she had enough food to last us through tomorrow, so she could put off having to ask Arun for more grocery money for another day.

As these dark thoughts swirled in her mind, it took her a moment to notice that the kitchen was darkening around her.

Chapati in hand, she watched in disbelief, certain that she was imagining it. But no, the light in the kitchen was slowly dimming. Looking out of the window, she saw the summer evening was still bright. Glancing up, she saw that the kitchen light was still switched on but wasn't illuminating the room as it should. She could see the lightbulb through the dark, like a streetlight through a thick fog.

How odd.

A prickly unease came over her, like a spider walking over bare skin. Then the temperature began to drop. It became noticeably colder and continued as though caused by a strong draft of cold air. Again, she looked to the window. The tiny part at the top was pushed open a few inches. She looked over at the kitchen door. Shut.

She felt the hairs raise on her arm and looked down to see goosebumps. Cold? Fear? She set her chapati back on the plate. Her stomach was in knots now. Turning to look at Arun, she saw he was also watching the darkening with astonishment. So, at least she knew she wasn't imagining it. Their eyes met briefly, each as perplexed as the other, before they looked away and continued to watch, with growing dread, as the kitchen inexorably darkened and cooled until they could hardly see beyond the table.

They sat in the dark for a few moments, paralysed with fear. *We should leave,* she thought. But she couldn't lift herself from the chair. She looked to see if I had noticed. I was still eating, seemingly oblivious and unaffected by the dark and the cold. She looked to a corner where the bin and brooms stood. Was that the outline of a person? She could almost make it out... but then she blinked and it was gone.

"What's happening?" Arun whisper-hissed beside her in his usual cross tone.

"I, I don't know," she answered, truthfully. It was hard to see beyond the table where they sat, but she strained to see through the dark.

She yelped as a shadow darted beside her, brushing her arm.

“Did you see that?” He whisper-hissed furiously again. “There’s something here.”

She couldn’t answer and only nodded.

“Where did it go?” He asked urgently in a low voice.

“I can’t see.” She replied.

The small kitchen felt larger now that they couldn’t see to the corners. A sound broke the silence.

Scratching. Like fingernails on a blackboard. She thought it was coming from the Formica worktop. A high-pitched whining sound. Her heart pounded and her legs trembled under the table.

“Do you hear that?” He asked in an accusing tone.

“Uh huh.” She answered. She leaned forward, straining to see with all her might.

“Oh my!” She breathed, her hand flying to her mouth to stifle a scream.

A figure rose from the dark to stand in front of the window, no distance from their table. The figure was darker than the room. It moved an arm. The scratching came again. A slow jagged drag.

She closed her eyes and felt like she was going to faint. She forced her eyes open. The figure moved towards them. Finally, flight mode kicked in. She turned to reach across the table to me, planning to grab me and get out. She looked at me and screamed.

An arm came out of the darkness behind me, and a hand wrapped itself around my throat. A woman's face moved into view over my head, her wild, maniacal eyes fixed on my mother. The woman was smoky grey, as if made of shadow itself, with long black hair that cascaded over her shoulders. As my mother watched in horror, the shadow woman tilted my head up and pulled me firmly back into my seat, with the back of my head pressed to her chest.

My mother couldn't breathe. She grabbed at her chest, heart pounding, breath quickening and eyes wide, her pulse thundering in her ears.

As she fought to keep calm, the woman raised her other arm, extended her hand and index finger and pointed over my shoulder to Arun.

Beside her, my mother could sense Arun saw her too and he was also terrified.

"How?" Arun said faintly beside her.

She forced herself to look directly at the woman's terrible face. She was Indian, like us; a young woman who could have been beautiful in life, but who was now clearly dead, with nothing beautiful left about her now.

The woman glared at my mother with eyes devoid of all reason, lips pulled back over rotted teeth, jaw tensed. Her outstretched hand raised and lowered in a deft movement, before pointing again at him.

Look, she seemed to convey. Look!

Who was she? What did she want? Priya tore her gaze from the woman's face to look at me. To her astonishment, I was calmly looking over her head, eyes fixed somewhere on the wall behind her, a relaxed smile on my face. As if I were in another kitchen entirely.

"How?" Arun was repeating faintly beside her. "What? How?"

Priya turned to him. Guilt and fear were etched on his face as he stared at the shadow woman in terror, mouth opening and closing like a fish gulping for air. Her stomach lurched. Cogs turned and puzzle pieces fell into place. She closed her eyes, feeling tears on her cheek.

"Is that Samira?" She asked breathlessly.

Arun turned to look at her then and nodded helplessly, his fear-filled eyes beseeching her to help him.

Hate twisted like a viper inside her. Her fists clenched. She looked back to the woman formed of shadow before her, whose hand was around her daughter's neck. The woman who was staring at her with dogged, desperate, determination. Arm outstretched, pointing accusingly to him.

LOOK! The woman silently screamed at her.

The shadow woman moved her arm from pointing at Arun to reaching out to Priya, palm up.

"Don't!" Priya heard him say.

She ignored him and, despite her fear, reached slowly out to take the shadow woman's hand. And then, the dam she'd been holding back all the years, exploded within her.

She had already been haunted by Samira, albeit metaphorically. In the run up to their arranged marriage in India, a marriage my mother had begged and pleaded to get out of, worrying tales of my father's first wife, Samira, were rife. Rumours were relayed to her, either as a cautionary tale by her friends, or told with gleeful relish by spiteful family members who cared not for her happiness.

At eighteen, Arun had married sixteen-year-old Samira, in a marriage arranged by their families. After a couple of years of marriage, they had a baby girl who remained their only child. Priya was told by all who had known, or known of, her new husband's original family that the marriage wasn't a happy one. The young bride often made excuses to return to her family home for weeks at a time. They didn't attend family events such as marriages or birthdays and rarely socialised or holidayed, despite being financially able.

Then tragedy struck. At just eleven years old, their daughter drowned in the bath. A sudden seizure or faint was blamed. It was Samira who found her. And when she did, she was so overcome with grief, she hung herself in the same bathroom. Arun found them both when he returned from work that evening, having had to force open the bathroom door. A double tragedy that rocked the local community and prompted a wave of sympathy.

Until the rumours started.

Samira's family urged the police to investigate thoroughly, accusing Arun of murder. The police brushed them off. The crime scene had been cleared with only half-hearted efforts to gather evidence, all of which supported Arun's version of events.

Arun spread his own rumours; that his wife was a depressive drunk, unfit to parent, who had left the girl on her own in the bath instead of looking after her properly.

She was eleven years old! His wife's family countered, angrily. She didn't need to be supervised in the bath like an infant. They said Samira had been mistreated by Arun for years and that she was planning to leave Arun and take her daughter with her. They said she'd had accused Arun of spending too much time with their daughter alone, showing 'unnatural affections.'

Unnatural affections.

That was the term the rumour mongers used when they retold the stories to Priya. The words were spoken slowly, in low tones, accompanied by knowing looks, to make her interpret the words darkly. As Priya watched me grow and change, these words would echo in her mind more often.

Unnatural affections.

Recently, out of the blue and entirely out of character, Arun had suggested Priya sign up for weekly aerobics classes he'd seen advertised in the community centre. He'd offered to pay for them, saying he would be home in time to allow her to go and that he could look after me for the evening.

In the normal course of the week, Arun and I spent no time alone together at all. It was so out of character, that despite the temptation to leave the house one evening a week to spend time with other adults and get some exercise, Priya declined his offer.

This had displeased him greatly. Why was that? She wondered. Arun did not like her, she reminded herself. He had her living almost in poverty, despite his seemingly good job. He always dressed well in smart clothes and quality shoes. He paid his membership to a local cricket club and socialised there often. Her cheap shoes were worn through, and she didn't have a proper coat for the Scottish winters. So why did he want her out of the house?

Unnatural affections.

How does an eleven-year-old girl drown in the bath?

Would suicide really be your first act upon finding your daughter drowned? Without even trying to phone an ambulance or raise the alarm?

Priya unclasped and pulled back her hand, dropping it to her side.

She opened her eyes and stared into the mad eyes of the young shadow woman whose hand was wrapped around her daughter's throat, all thoughts and memories having coalesced in seconds.

A wave of tranquillity washed over Priya like a warm wave on a sunny beach.

She breathed in deeply and exhaled.

All her underlying anxiety evaporated, leaving only peace and purpose.

"I understand now," she said to the shadow woman before her.

Samira leaned back, her eyes less mad, but no less determined. Gently, Samira released my throat. My mother stood up from the table and Samira moved to stand beside her. The women smiled at each other, like they were old friends.

Watching them, Arun started to panic in earnest. Knocking over his chair, he stood and bolted to the kitchen door.

Calmly, Priya walked over to the kitchen counter and lifted the heavy rolling pin she'd used for the chapatis.

Then, together, she and Samira slowly followed Arun out of the kitchen, through the living room, to the small hallway and the front door. There, they found him frantically trying to undo the deadbolts he'd installed on the door with shaking hands.

He didn't hear his two wives step behind him.

Gripping the rolling pin with both hands, Priya raised it above her head. With a strength she didn't know she could muster, she brought it down, hard, on the crown of his head.

It made a sickening crack.

As did the next blow.

And the one after that.

Samira touched Priya's arm to signal that she should stop. Priya smiled at her, eager to please. They watched him in companionable silence for a few moments as he lay the floor before them, bleeding and unconscious.

Priya looked at Samira again. *What now?* She asked, without speaking.

Samira pointed down the hall, to the open bathroom door.

Yes, of course. Priya dropped the rolling pin to the floor, picked her bleeding husband up by the armpits, and with surprising ease dragged him down the hall. Once in the bathroom, she closed the door and again looked to Samira for guidance. Samira pointed to Arun's bathrobe, hanging on a hook on the inside of the door.

How fitting, Priya thought with a smile. She slipped the belt out of the bathrobe and looped it tightly around Arun's neck. Awkwardly, she sat him up and pushed his back against the inside of the bathroom door. She reached up and tied the other end of the belt around the hook the bathrobe still hung on.

With Samira at her side, she calmly knelt before her unconscious husband and, as she looked at his face, she felt Samira place her hand on her shoulder.

A renewed feeling of peace flooded through her, like a ray of light piercing the clouds.

Then, she pulled her husband forward into her arms. She arched back as far as the taut belt around his neck allowed them, pulling with all her might.

Feeling the life leave his body felt euphoric, peaceful, and right. She held him for untold moments in that macabre embrace until, at last, the high began to wane. Eventually, she let him fall from her arms and stood up. He slumped to the side, and she was able to pull the door open just enough to step through it.

Priya entered the hallway alone.

The sound of the door closing behind her made her jump.

How did she get to the hall?

She looked to see if there was someone beside her. There wasn't.

Why did she think there would be?

She shook her head. As she walked back down the hall, she felt dizzy and disorientated.

She saw blood stains and a bloodied rolling pin on the hallway floor and started to panic. What had happened? Who was bleeding? Where was Ameera? She shook her head again, trying to clear her mind.

Upon entering the kitchen, she saw it was light again. Why did she think it would be dark?

She tried to focus on me. I was staring at the wall, laughing softly. “Ameera,” she said. I didn’t respond.

“Ameera!” she repeated, sharply. “What are you looking at?"

I jumped and looked around at her before looking back at the wall again, my face twisted in confusion. "Where did she go?” I asked, in a panic. “There was a girl, just there.” I pointed at the wall. “She was just there, I swear!"

We looked at each other as the mists slowly cleared, and we each tried to shake ourselves back into reality.

"What? What girl?” Priya asked me.

“She looked a bit like me. But taller. She was right there!” I insisted, close to tears.

I looked around the room unhappily, before asking, “Where’s Dad?”

Just like that, the fog cleared and the memory of what had just happened hit my mother like a spade in the face.

Horrified, she sprinted out of the kitchen, through the living room, and down the hall to the bathroom. The bathroom door was closed.

Revulsion and panic washed over her. She didn't want to open the door. No, no, no. It couldn't be true.

Steeling herself, she started to force the door open, struggling against the weight of Arun. When she got the door open enough to squeeze through. She was met with the sight of Arun's mottled, purple face staring up at her, swollen and caked with blood. She vomited so violently she missed the toilet. Frantically, with shaking hands, she untied the belt from his neck, smacking his cheek and calling his name.

This wasn't happening. She heard screaming and looked up to see me watching her, my face contorted in horror. I paused to inhale, then kept screaming. The neighbours would be here soon. What to do? What to do? Her thoughts raced before she steeled herself and decided to go on the offensive.

First, she put me in my room out of the way and instructed me to stay there. Then she cleaned the hall and hid the bloody towels and rolling pin above a wardrobe. Ready, she opened the front door and yelled, "Help me! Someone call an ambulance!"

Neighbours arrived in moments. Someone took me to their flat, and someone else called 999. The police arrived and started CPR until the ambulance came. Arun was pronounced dead at the scene.

Despite the deep shock she felt, survival mode stilled her thoughts, and my mother cobbled together an explanation.

Through sobs, and in broken English, she told the kindly police officers her husband had arrived home from work bloodied and distraught. He said he'd been jumped by a group of skinheads who'd pushed him around, called him 'Paki' and told him to 'go home.' As he'd fled from them, one had thrown a brick at the back of his head. He'd arrived home bleeding, shaken, and in tears. He couldn't be calmed, saying he couldn't take it anymore. She'd implored him to ring and report the assault. He refused, saying he'd be targeted even more if he did. She'd begged him to call an ambulance. Again, he refused, saying the cut wasn't as bad as it seemed.

Reluctantly, she agreed to make his dinner while he went to the bathroom to get cleaned up, so that I wouldn't see him. After twenty minutes or so, she'd become worried and had gone to check on him, having to force the door to get in. When she'd found him hanged and couldn't revive him, she'd screamed for help. The police listened sympathetically to the small Asian woman in front of them while trying to follow her story. When the scene had been cleared and the body taken to the morgue, they asked if she had anyone she could call, or anywhere else to stay. She said no, but that she would be fine here with her neighbours and thanked the police for their kindness.

The next few weeks passed slowly. She disposed of the rolling pin and towels easily enough, stashing them in one of the many piles of rubbish on the estate. She stuck to her story and, apart from giving a lengthier statement a day or so later, she wasn't questioned too closely. Rumours of Arun's death and the preceding 'attack' circulated. Instead of it being disputed or debunked as she had feared, the people of the estate seemed to rally around the unfortunate family.

Witnesses came forward to say they too had seen the skinheads, and/or been harassed by them. There was even a witness to the 'assault.' He was a local drunk, well known to the police. He claimed he'd not only seen it, but that he'd helped Arun fight them off! The police may not have believed him or regarded him as a credible witness. But crucially, they didn't find any reason to dispute my mother's version of events. She could've been caught out by the police in a number of ways; from neighbours telling them Arun arrived home unbloodied and earlier than claimed, to the police realising Priya was well educated and spoke fluent English. But the days and weeks crawled past, and no one came to challenge her.

Only her mother and father, grandparents I'd never met, came over for Arun's funeral. They were self-aware enough not to express regret for her loss. Her father had the good grace to look guilty, even if he wouldn't apologise outright for the marriage he had strong-armed his daughter into. They half-heartedly tried to build a relationship with me, but I was uninterested. Where had they been when we needed them? Even at that age, I knew they were responsible for the life we led. They didn't stay long. I went back to school a few days after the funeral. Priya and I deliberately didn't speak about the night of Arun's death. But our alliance endured, and we were closer than ever. As she navigated informing Arun's work, bank, etc, of his untimely demise, she received good news.

We had money! What he was saving for, and why we lived on that shitty estate, she would never know. There were thousands in the bank. Tens of thousands!

Her parents asked her to return home. But no, India was no longer our home. Glasgow wasn't home either. She investigated a few options and decided Belfast was the sweet spot of being cheap to live in and far enough from Glasgow, its bad memories and the Glaswegian police. Priya told the police she was returning to India and gave them her parents' address in Mumbai. They promised to keep her 'abreast of developments.' Unsurprisingly, we didn't hear from them again.

After Arun's death, Priya felt like she was living two lives. In one, she knew ghosts were real and that one had helped her murder her husband in cold blood. Something she didn't regret at all, but at times couldn't quite believe. In that life, she should, by rights, have been in jail.

In her other life, she was a grieving widow who'd lost her husband to suicide. A brave, single, immigrant widow who everyone was sympathetic to. She felt she was entitled to a little sympathy by then.

As she tried not to go crazy, she reached out to her parents in Mumbai and asked if they could try to locate any old photos of Arun's first family. She said I was struggling with the loss of my father and wanted to know more about him and his old life in India.

Priya's parents had been in touch with some of Arun's remaining family following his death, so procuring some photos of him wasn't difficult. They sent her an envelope by recorded delivery, filled with photos; photos from his first wedding, the birth of his daughter, right up to the last photo taken of his daughter before she died. She had never seen photos of Samira before but, without a doubt, the woman in the photos was the shadow woman from the kitchen that fateful night.

Once she knew the truth, she stopped living two lives and accepted it. Ghosts were real, and one had helped her escape the man who had ruined both their lives. She gave thanks to Samira almost every day, burning incense and offering prayers. She often felt her presence, and when she did, she felt reassured and protected."

Chapter 13

The Gathering, 22:00

The mood at the table is sombre once again. Ameera pushes her wine glass away from her with a trembling hand. She is crying silently. No one seems to know what to say. LA pulls her handbag onto her lap. I follow her gaze out the window and realise it has started to rain. I sigh, remembering I need to bus it home and wondering how much a taxi would cost at this time of night. I look around the table and see Lydia is tearful too. Maybe retelling the events surrounding her lost pregnancies is too much for her.

Again, I wonder at the purpose of these evenings. Everyone's story is so bloody sad and upsetting! I feel wrung out listening to these unhappy tales. Does no one have a happy ending? God, I wish I'd never been invited. I should have stood up to Joanna and said I wasn't coming. Why could I not say no to this woman? I am always rearranging cleaning slots with others to accommodate her, when half the time she doesn't even have the cash in hand to pay me and I have to wait longer while she 'pops to the ATM', arriving home with bags of shopping, completely oblivious to the fact she's wasting my time by keeping me waiting.

Looking at my watch, I see it's ten o'clock. I wonder what time these 'Gatherings' normally end. There seems to be an unspoken consensus that the night is over. We've all had enough.

"Well, I for one have had enough for one night. And I don't just mean the wine!" Lydia says, her voice breaking.

"Yes, I think that might do us. What do you think, Ameera?" Joanna asks, looking pointedly to Ameera for approval.

Don't the rest of us get a say?

LA pipes up apologetically, "I actually have to be in court at nine."

"No! No! No!" shouts Eleanor, banging the table. "NO! I've just been telling whatserface over here," she pauses and waves her fingers at me, "about poor Ada and her sickness. Can we not tell one of her stories, seeing as how she isn't here to tell it herself, poor soul? It's a nice way to include her. We can't just forget about her. And it's the only story some of us are in together. We always tell it!" she whines. "And I don't have court in the morning and I'm in serious need of more wine."

She stands and lurches over to the counter, grabbing a few bottles before weaving her way back to the table, grabbing some nibbles as she goes. LA rolls her eyes at Lydia. They both look furious.

Sarah, Ameera and Joanna all appear to be communicating silently. All wide eyes, tight smiles and raised eyebrows.

Of course, no one gives a shit what I want. "I really need to be heading on now. Thanks for a lov..." I start.

Ameera and Joanna each grab one of my hands, squeezing them tightly. "Absolutely not." "Not yet." They say in unison. Joanna forces a laugh.

Annoyed, I yank my hands free.

Joanna brightens her face which has been twisted in a scowl. "Ameera will be driving past your house on her way home – she's going to give you a lift."

"There! It's decided." Ameera adds.

A lift home in the rain sounds good. Fuck it, only one more tale to go. I push my glass towards Eleanor to get it refilled.

Joanna smiles and looks around the table theatrically, clearly delighted to be the centre of attention. "Okay! Last one. Some of you feature in this story, so do interrupt me if I get it wrong."

Chapter 14

Joanna's Story – 'The Many-Faced Friend'

~~~

Joanna: *I hadn't planned on retelling my tale tonight, but I suppose it's only fair. Besides, it will prolong the evening and its ending for a while longer.*

Ameera looks close to losing her nerve.

I haven't kept track of Sarah's drinking. She'd better not be half cut.

LA and Eleanor are full as usual.

And bloody Eleanor can't stop babbling about Ada. We don't need her to be in the forefront of our minds - tonight of all nights.

Lydia is her usual ray of sunshine self. Good grief, would it kill her to be nice? Or not be so brutally honest?

I'd better not think too much about M. We need to see this through to the end.

Only my tale left to go.

I'd best get on with it.

~~~

"My Mum didn't like to admit it, but getting pregnant in her forties wasn't planned. It was 1991. I was eleven years old, Sean was twelve, and Nuala was nearly five and had just started primary school. This had freed Mum up to return to work and earn some much-needed extra money. So, when she found out she was pregnant with twins, she was gutted. I think she was the talk of the place.

We weren't poor, exactly. Dad worked as a teacher and was always good with money. I don't remember missing meals or anything like that. But money was definitely tight. Mum made a lot of our clothes, the heat wasn't on much and there weren't many treats or holidays. Donegal, if we were lucky.

Our house at the time was a smallish semi-detached in South Belfast. Mum and Dad had the biggest bedroom, of course. Nuala and I shared the next biggest, and Sean had a boxroom you couldn't swing a cat in. Selfish brats that we were, the first thing we asked when they told us Mum was pregnant with twins was, "Where are you going to put them?"

Mum had sailed through our pregnancies, but this pregnancy was really hard on her. She was sick every morning the entire time and towards the end the twins stopped gaining weight. They induced her early one morning at thirty-five weeks pregnant.

Ada came into the world first, weighing just under four pounds.

Edward's birth was trickier and took another couple of hours. He weighed barely three pounds when he finally arrived. Mum said afterwards, that if she had been a first-time mother, the staff would have monitored her, and her newborns, more closely. As it was, the busy nurses left her alone with both babies, even though she was exhausted from all the sickness and a gruelling induced labour. Dad stayed with her in the morning but had to rush off to do the school run. He planned to come back with us in tow in the evening. When Mum tried to say something wasn't right with Edward, the nurses dismissed her concerns, attributing his fatigue to the tough birth. Exhausted, Mum fell asleep around noon. Something she never forgave herself for.

When Ada's cries woke her around three pm, she realised Edward was unresponsive. The alarm was finally raised, and everyone swung urgently into action. But it was too late. Edward's blood sugars had plummeted, and his tiny body didn't recover. He passed away that evening, aged just one day old.

It was a brutal time for Mum and Dad. They had a long and complex inquest to deal with, crippling guilt, a newborn daughter, and us lot. I honestly don't know how they got through it. I guess life goes on.

Ada was a great wee toddler. Whereas the rest of us were blonde like Mum, Ada had a shock of red hair like Dad, and it matched her fiery personality. She and Nuala were thick as thieves and she was always torturing Sean and me for attention, running and jumping on us the minute we'd get in from school. She was a wee daredevil, loving rough horseplay and doing zoomie style laps of the garden on her scooter. She never stopped talking from the minute she woke until she said her bedtime prayers.

Ada knew she was a twin and that her brother had died young. There was a lone mass card with a tiny photo of Edward high on a shelf. You couldn't keep something that big a secret. But we didn't talk about Edward much; it was just too painful. So, when Ada started talking about her imaginary friend, 'Teddy' when she was three years old, it was unexpected. No one had ever called Edward 'Teddy,' but there he suddenly was. Or rather, there he wasn't.

It started with the usual imaginary friend stuff. We'd hear her playing in her room making one half of a conversation. She'd ask Teddy if he wanted dinner, offer him her snacks, and ask him to go to the park with her - that sort of thing.

We'd wind her up, going to fetch one of her teddies and asking if this was who she was talking to. But she'd always get annoyed and say "No!" and that "Teddy was her friend."

Mum and Dad didn't love it at first. They didn't think it was healthy for her to be 'talking' to her dead twin but there was no stopping her. In the end, they sort of embraced it as a nice way for her to remember Edward.

As kids, we thought it was sweet, and, as she was such a handful, it was nice to get a break from her attentions when she spent time chatting to and playing with Teddy. We heard Ada talking to Teddy so often, we started talking to him too.

We'd shout, "Ada and Teddy need their shoes on in two minutes or they're not going for ice-cream!" Ada would jump up, shout "Come quick!" hold out her hand and go tearing off to her room, Teddy in tow. Or, we'd say, "Teddy's tired, you need to go to bed now" and she'd say, "Come on, Teddy" and toddle off to bed, holding out her elbow as if she and Teddy were linking arms.

It was ridiculously cute. Until it wasn't.

When I was about fifteen, I was a hormonal grump. Overconfident and argumentative. Ada would have been four by then and Teddy had been around for over a year, when something odd happened.

I was sitting at Mum's dressing table one day practising putting on her makeup, no doubt looking like a child prostitute, when I heard Ada outside the door.

"No! I don't want to tell her." She whispered in a harsh voice.

"Don't want to tell me what?" I shouted out to her.

"No! I am not saying it!" She loud whispered again.

Irritated now, I turned to the empty doorway. "What aren't you saying?" I snapped.

Ada sidled into the doorframe looking furtively to her left, the direction she'd come from.

"Well, what is it?" I demanded, hands on hips.

She looked at her feet and mumbled incomprehensibly. All I could make out was 'Mr Wilson.' Mr Wilson was my Technology and Design teacher at school.

"Jesus Christ, Ada, what the hell do you know about Mr Wilson?"

Looking close to tears, Ada said in a shaky voice, "Teddy says Mr Wilson plays with his winky in the storeroom after he talks to you in class."

My stomach dropped. "What did you just say?" I asked in disbelief.

"There! I said it. I'm not saying any more." She shouted before she raced off to the box room she'd inherited from Sean after Mum and Dad converted the attic and moved him up into it a few years before. Indignant, I followed her down the hall, ready to tell her off.

But I felt sick. Mr Wilson was well known for being the school perv. I didn't like how he looked at me, or how he'd offer to help me in class by wrapping his arms around me to slowly tie my apron strings.

"How do you even know who Mr Wilson is?" I barked at her when I reached her door. "Did our Sean mention him?"

"No." Ada said sadly, sitting on the floor beside her bed with her arms wrapped around her legs.

"And what do you mean he plays with his winky?!" I hissed at her, not wanting Mum or Dad to hear us.

She shrugged, a picture of misery. "I dunno what playing with his winky means. That's just what Teddy told me to tell you." She answered, looking at the corner of the room guiltily.

I glanced at the corner. There was nothing there but shoes and discarded clothes. I looked back at Ada. She was still looking to the corner while slowly nodding her head. A creepy feeling came over me. Suddenly, I felt sure we weren't alone in the room. I told myself I was being silly and chided myself for letting her talk of Teddy get to me.

"Don't say stuff like that again, Ada. And don't go blaming Teddy either. You hear me?" I said, trying to keep the worry out of my voice.

Ada dropped her head and nodded again. I turned back to the hall.

Bang! I jumped as her bedroom door immediately slammed shut behind me. I burst back into her room to give out to her.

"You wee Madam!" I roared. But she was sitting in exactly the same spot as before; not standing behind the door as I'd expected. Looking closely at her, I saw she was breathing heavily, her hands were balled into fists at her side with her fingernails digging into her palms. Her cheeks were puffing in and out, and her eyes were full of tears as she stared straight ahead.

"Ada?" I said in a kinder tone. Again, I had the strong sensation we weren't alone. I looked to the corner again. Nothing. I fought to stay calm.

Could Ada have jumped up, slammed the door and sat back down in the few seconds it had taken for the door to slam behind me and for me to open it? It seemed unlikely, but not impossible.

"Why don't you come downstairs with me?" I asked her gently.

She glanced to the corner, then shook her head.

Still looking at the corner I reached out my hand. "Ada, you need to come downstairs with me now. Come on."

Reluctantly, she rose off the ground, took my hand and allowed herself to be led out of the room. Once downstairs, I left her in the sitting room with Nuala and fetched us both a drink as a peace offering. When I brought it back to her, she was curled up asleep, with her head on Nuala's lap. The moment was lost, and we never did discuss what she said about Mr Wilson.

A few weeks later, I was doing homework at the dining table when I heard Sean shouting angrily at Ada upstairs. I listened for a few moments to see if it would blow over, but Sean was getting more and more riled up as he bawled her out. As Mum and Dad weren't home, I went up to see what was going on. Sean was apoplectic! His face was purple, and he was screaming at the top of his lungs about liars and punishments. When he saw me, he pointed to me and roared at Ada, "GO WITH JOANNA AND GET THE FUCK OUT OF MY FACE, YOU LYIN' WEE BITCH!!"

Jesus! Ada sprinted out of her room, down the hall towards me and dashed down the stairs, looking upset.

"That wee bitch!" Sean spat. "Saying all sorts of shit an' blaming fuckin' Teddy. I'll whip her arse if she speaks to me like that again. I don't care if she's wee!"

"What did she say?" I asked.

"Stuff she shouldn't fuckin know at her age!" He stormed, before stomping up the stairs to his room in the attic.

Knowing better than to bother him when he was this angry, I went downstairs to find Ada. She was in the kitchen, standing with her head pressed to a cupboard door. I hovered in the doorway, not sure if she'd seen me. "Are you happy now?" She asked in a small voice.

"Happy about what?" I asked.

She jumped and spun round to look at me, clearly oblivious to my presence.

"Were you talking to Teddy?" I asked her, looking round the room. "Did he tell you to tell our Sean something?"

Ada looked to the floor and nodded.

"What was it?" I asked, looking round the kitchen. Again, it felt as if someone else was there with us.

"Oh, I am not saying *that* again," she said defiantly.

"Fine. But you have to stop this, Ada, d'ya hear me?" I said, trying to sound more confident than I felt. "And you need to apologise to Sean. Okay?"

Ada just shrugged, looking defeated.

Mum and Dad hoped she'd have grown out of 'Teddy talk' by the time she started school. Ada hadn't been a great one for interacting with other kids. In the park or at family events, she tended to cling to us or chat with Teddy. Most kids can't wait to start school but Ada wasn't keen. One sunny August evening, we were all in the garden, sitting on the outdoor furniture having a BBQ, when Mum raised the subject with her.

"Do you think Teddy will miss you when you go to school next week, Ada?" She asked lightly.

"Why would Teddy not be at school?" Answered Ada, tucking into her charred corn on the cob.

"Imaginary friends don't become imaginary pupils." Mum explained, "And the other kids might laugh at you. Wouldn't it be nice to make some new friends? Some real friends?"

"Ah, you'll get so bullied if you introduce your imaginary dead twin brother to your new school friends. How creepy is that?" Laughed Sean, who was an insensitive, spotty sixteen-year-old by now.

"Teddy's not my brother. Why do you all think that?" Ada answered crossly. "He's my friend and he says he's the only friend I need, and he'll be at school with me because he's always everywhere with me! Even when I tell him I don't want him to be with me, he's still with me." She paused, a guilty look on her face, as if she'd said too much. She looked down and slowly started eating her corn on the cob again, but we could tell it was to avoid the conversation.

We all made eyes at each other while she stared at her plate.

Kindly, Mum asked her. "When do you tell Teddy you don't want him to be with you?"

Ada munched thoughtfully for a moment, then looked around the garden before answering. "Like sometimes at night when he won't stop talking and I'm too tired. Or, if I want to talk to someone else and he doesn't want me to."

"If he's really your friend, why would Teddy not want you to talk to anyone else?" Mum pressed, gently.

"Because *he* can't. And if *he* can't talk to other people then it's not fair that *I* talk to other people."

Again, we made eyes at each other.

Mum took the lead. "What happens if you *do* talk to other people?"

"He gets cross."

"Oh dear. And what happens when he gets cross?"

"I'm not supposed to say."

"Why not? Did he tell you not to tell us?"

"Well, no. Not quite."

"Well, there you are honey. What happens when he gets cross?"

"Urgh!" Exclaimed Ada, throwing the corn husk down on her plate. "It's awful! When he's playing nice, he's as big as me and his face is a boy's. When he's not playing nice, he takes the boy face off and gets big. That's when he has the *other* face. The one I don't like. If I do what he tells me to do, he puts the boy face back on and becomes wee again, like me."

We all looked at each other in confusion. What on earth?

"Is he here now?" Asked Mum, worry creeping into her voice.

"No. He doesn't like it when there are too many of you in one place. I can't see or hear him properly." Her head shot up then, eyes full of worry. "You won't tell him I told you about him, will you? I'm not supposed to talk about him."

"Of course not, honey," answered Mum, making wide, mad eyes at Dad.

Sighing, Dad put down his knife and fork and called Ada over to him. She doted on Dad and happily ran round to jump up on his knee. Dad cuddled her close, stroking her hair. "Now! I don't like to hear that people get cross with my wee princess. Do I need to bop this fella on the nose?" He made a fist and started making punching motions in the air.

Ada laughed and tried to catch his hand. "No silly. Sure, you can't see him. How would you hit him."

"Clever Daddy has a plan for that. You tell me where he is, and I'll give him a good gubbing. How does that sound?" Dad said, tickling Ada and still miming punching the air. "Eh?"

"You'll have to punch higher than that, Dad. When he's not wee like me, he's bigger than you."

Dad locked eyes with Mum. "Is he indeed?"

After Mum got Ada down to sleep that night, we all discussed Teddy in the living room. No one could remember for sure if Ada had ever actually said he was her brother. And we couldn't remember if she'd ever said he was a kid like her either. Maybe we'd just assumed he was because they did kid stuff together and, well, you assume a four-year-old's imaginary friend is an imaginary four-year-old.

"Do you think she should go and see someone?" Dad asked Mum. "Playing with and talking to a friendly imaginary brother/boy whatever is one thing. Talking to something who tells you who you can and can't talk to, grows big and who pulls it's fecking face off, is quite another."

"Let's not panic. I know she's nervous about starting school. Maybe once she goes, she'll grow out of all this Teddy nonsense." Mum answered, keen as ever not to make a fuss.

We all agreed to pay more attention to Teddy and share what we heard. A couple of nights after the BBQ, Nuala and I were crouched at our bedroom door when Ada was in her room alone, so she couldn't see us while we eavesdropped.

"Dinner is chicken nuggets, oven chips and peas." We heard her say. "Is so! I asked Mum like you told me to and that's what she said!"

Nuala and I rolled our eyes at each other, already bored.

"But I like chips. I want to eat them." Ada continued.

We squinted at each other, heads cocked.

"No! Mum will shout at me if I don't, then go on and on about the starving kids in Africa."

Nuala and I started to giggle and covered our mouths with our hands.

"OW!" Yelled Ada.

Startled, we rushed in to find her nursing her arm, her face twisted in pain.

"What happened?" Nuala asked her, pulling her into a hug.

"Nothin'," Ada answered unhappily, fighting back the tears.

I stared around her room. It didn't feel right. It reminded me of the time I thought someone else was in the room with us. "Did Teddy hurt you?" I asked her.

"No! What makes you say that?" She shouted at me.

"What happened to your arm?" Asked Nuala. "How did you get that red mark?"

"And why was he telling you not to eat chips?" I asked.

"He wasn't! Stop lying!" Ada bellowed at us, before running out of the room and hurtling downstairs. Nuala chased after her, calling her name.

I stayed in her room, looking around. Something felt really off. What was it? I looked down at my arm. The hairs on it were raised. Ada's room was cold. Noticeably colder than our room. Was that it? Not quite. It was that same creepy feeling from before, like there was something else in the room with me. Slowly, I rotated on the spot and looked around the room. Nothing looked out of order. I shook myself and took a step towards the door.

Whump.

A soft sound came from behind me. I turned to see a stuffed dog lying on the floor beside Ada's bed. Ada always had about twenty toys on her bed at one time, one must have fallen, I guessed. But the dog hadn't been on the floor when I looked around the room. Or had it? More likely, I just hadn't noticed it. It must have been on the edge of the bed and just slid off. I moved towards the door again, not wanting to be alone in her room anymore.

Swoosh, click. The door smoothly swung itself shut before I could get to it.

I stood in front of it, heart thumping. Tears pricked my eyes.

Whump!

The sound was louder this time. Slowly, I turned around.

A large doll with plastic limbs and head was now lying beside the stuffed dog. That doll hadn't been on the edge of the bed, it had been on the pillow.

I looked at the pillow where a crowd of toys lay in a tumble. To my amazement, a purple My Little Unicorn started to slide off the pillow and move slowly to the edge of the bed.

I was really scared now, frozen to the spot, wide eyed, heart racing. My instincts told me to look more closely at the pile of toys on the pillow. I didn't want to, but I forced myself to take my eyes off the unicorn and look up at the top of the bed.

Oh my God!

In the middle of the toy pile, I saw the back of a head with greasy, matted black hair. As my eyes tried to comprehend what I was seeing, to my horror, the shape of a man's body lifted beneath the sheets in Ada's single bed, like the bed had taken a breath and blown out the shape of it.

I squealed and backed up to the shut door, trying the handle.

It didn't turn.

The body began to rouse itself. The shoulder shifted and I saw the shape of an arm lift under the sheet. Still facing away from me, the torso began to rise up.

Frantic, I tried the doorknob again. It still wouldn't open. Crying now, I couldn't tear my eyes from the back of the head. It started to turn towards me. I saw the outline of an ear, hideous hide-like skin on its cheek.

My legs buckled and I screamed. In a blind panic, I turned my back on the bed and wrenched at the doorknob in earnest.

Mercifully, it turned. I swung the door open and sprinted down to the living room.

I wanted to burst in and tell everyone what had happened, but I walked in on a blazing argument between Mum, Dad and Nuala.

Nuala was in tears, saying over and over that she hadn't hurt Ada.

"Then why does she say that you did?!" Mum yelled at her. "Apologise! Right now!"

I looked at Ada. She was staring unhappily at the floor. I took Ada by the shoulder and steered her into the kitchen, leaving the others to their row.

I took a moment to get my breath. “Teddy isn’t imaginary, is he?” I asked her.

Ada looked up at me, eyes filled with tears. She shook her head, a picture of misery.

“No. He’s real. And he’s really scary. I don’t want to be his friend anymore.”

“I believe you.” I said, pulling her into a hug. “It’s okay, don’t cry. We’ll figure this out.”

I had no clue how to figure it out.

Telling Mum and Dad didn’t feel like an option. They wouldn’t believe me. I didn’t want to tell Nuala either, she was only ten and still scared of the dark.

That left our Sean. Pain in the hole Sean. I took him aside that night and told him what happened.

“Fuck off!” He said, a huge grin on his face. “You’re sayin’ Teddy’s fuckin’ real? And he’s not Edward?”

“You know, just because you’re old enough to swear doesn’t mean you have to put a swear word in every sentence.” I chided him.

“Why the fuck not?” He grinned.

“Are you going to help me?” I pleaded.

“Help you do what?” He asked.

"Help me make Mum and Dad see that 'Teddy' is not some innocent imaginary friend! We have to get rid of it!"

"How the fuck would we do that?"

"I don't bloody know! But we have to do something. It's in our house! It tried to scare me, and it hurt wee Ada."

"You know, just because you can swear, doesn't mean..."

"Oh, fuck off Sean."

In the end, he agreed to help me but had no more ideas than I did. I was just grateful that he believed me.

Things trundled along, summer ended and the new school term started. Sean and I were at the same secondary school. Ada went to the same local primary school with Nuala, the one Sean and I had both attended. It was a lovely old school, with a red brick building that was over one hundred years old. We'd all enjoyed our time there.

Not Ada. It was a battle to get her in every morning and the teachers said she wasn't participating in class. She kept laying her head on her folded arms on the table, saying her head hurt too much to learn. In the evenings, she wasn't much better. She refused to do homework, ate like a bird and kept asking to go to bed. Mum and Dad took her to the doctor for blood tests, but everything looked normal.

We tried everything we could think of to cheer her up; trips to the park, games nights, walks to the ice cream shop, and going to Granny's house. Nothing worked. Ada looked miserable. It was pitiful to watch. Who knows a miserable five-year-old? Sean and I spoke often about her. Even he, who couldn't stop looking at himself in the mirror, noticed how wretched she'd become.

Eventually, it was Sean who suggested the Ouija board.

"I dunno, Sean. I don't want to speak to Teddy. Couldn't we get a priest round instead?"

"Think about it, Jo. Only you and Ada know it's real. Maybe it's someone who died in this house? We'll find out who it is, tell Mum and Dad, and then they can get rid of it. Yes?"

"No!"

But Sean was adamant and once the idea took root, there was no deterring him. A few days later, Lydia, Ameera and I were in my living room watching *Neighbours* and *Home and Away* after school. After seeing the man-shape in the bed, I'd insisted they came home with me as I didn't want to be home alone. I hadn't told them why.

Sean came into the room, full of swagger and reeking of CK One.

“Fuck off, Sean.” We chorused as one.

“Charming!” Sean grinned, arranging himself on the arm of a sofa beside Ameera, who he’d fancied for years. “Did you tell them yet, Jo?”

“Seriously, fuck off, Sean.” I said crossly.

“I’ll take that as a ‘No’ sister dearest. Which means I’ll need to be the one who tells them the sad saga of Ada’s scary, multi-faced, imaginary man-friend.”

“Tell us the wha ‘bout the wha?” Asked Lydia, her face screwed up.

“Don’t even ask,” I chided her. “You don’t want to know.”

“What don’t we want to know?” Asked Ameera, looking up at Sean.

“Oh, it’s a mighty tale, ladies. You’d better gather round...”

And so, to my annoyance, Sean told them everything while they listened, transfixed. Sean was always a prick, but he was a charismatic prick when he wanted to be. When he finished, Lydia and Ameera turned to me with eyes like saucers.

“Is that true?” Asked Ameera.

"I don't believe a word of it," said Lydia, bossily.

"But you're the one with the supposedly haunted house!" I exclaimed.

"Well?" Demanded Ameera.

"Well... yes. Sean's exaggerated here and there, but it mostly true." I admitted.

"So, you *do* think Mr Wilson wanks off after talking to you?" Sean sniggered. He laughed while I rolled my eyes.

"Well, obviously I don't know if that part is true!" I said, raging with Sean for sharing that detail and raging with myself for telling him in the first place. "But that's what Ada said Teddy told her to tell me. And I don't know how she would even know who Mr Wilson is."

"Wouldn't surprise me." Ameera said. "Did you see him spend ages 'rubbing lint off' Helen McHugh's apron, clearly copping a feel of her boobs the other day?"

"Don't blame him. Helen's boobs are legendary," said Sean, earning a thump on the arm from Ameera. "But back to the Teddy conundrum. We need your help to get him to move on to the other side, or at least to some other house on the street."

"What do you need our help for?" Lydia asked.

“Thought you’d never ask,” Sean beamed, before outlining his plan to use a Ouija board to contact Teddy, glean some knowledge about him and use it to our advantage.

“Why do *we* need to be here?” Ameera asked, clearly not keen on the idea. “Can’t you two do it?”

“I’ve done some extensive research,” Sean began, before being interrupted by Lydia snorting loudly. “As I was saying,” he continued, giving Lydia some serious side-eye, “I’ve done some extensive research down at the library, and Ouija’s work best with larger numbers. We’d create a bigger beacon or generate more energy to allow the entity to communicate. Or some shit.”

Three dubious faces looked back at him.

“Well, obviously you’ll need me here,” Lydia sighed.

“That’s obvious…how?” Retorted Ameera.

“Well, I already see spirits, so it’ll be attracted to me. Plus, I’m not scared of spirits, so I’ll not run away like Joanna did. And, most importantly, I’ll bring my Ouija board.” Lydia answered.

“You have a Ouija board?” I asked, sceptically.

“Oui. Ja. I sure do. It was my Aunt Rose’s. She was a famed Medium in her day. Mum didn’t like to bin it. It's in our attic, somewhere. I'll dig it out." Lydia answered in a haughty, bored tone.

Reluctantly, Ameera allowed Sean to talk her into it too. And just like that, we had a plan. What we needed next was a date.

It took a few weeks before Sean and I talked Mum and Dad into letting us mind the wee ones for the night and let them go for dinner. I told them I was having a few friends round and promised there'd be no booze.

Mum eyed us suspiciously as we gathered around to wave them off for the night. "And no drugs either. Or boys!" She yelled before getting into the taxi where Dad was waiting impatiently.

When the door shut, all eyes turned to Lydia. Theatrically, she pulled the Ouija board out of her backpack.

"Let's go girls!" she said in her best Shania voice, inciting a squeal from Ameera.

While Lydia, Sean and Ameera headed to the kitchen to get ready, I popped upstairs to check Ada and Nuala were still asleep. To get them to sleep quicker, Mum had allowed Ada to sleep in Nuala's bed, top to toe. I tiptoed over to check on both of them. They were dead to the world.

As I softly closed the door behind me, I looked at the closed door of the box room and shivered, remembering the body in the bed.

Was this a terrible idea? I asked myself. No one else really knew for sure that Teddy was real, and to quote Ada, 'really scary', apart from me. What if something bad happened? No. This had to stop. I couldn't keep living in fear and we had to get it away from wee Ada.

"Fuck's keepin' ya, Jo?" Sean shouted from the kitchen.

I took a deep breath and padded down the stairs to join the others. Lydia, Ameera and Sean were sitting at our dining table, Lydia and Ameera on one side, Sean on the other. The lights were off, and four candles were lit on the table. I sat down beside Sean.

The Ouija board sat in the centre of the table with an upside-down glass tumbler in the middle of it. Suddenly, it looked ominous.

"Now what?" Asked Ameera.

"Everyone, touch the glass." Lydia instructed.

Nervously, we all reached out our arms and gently placed a finger on the tumbler.

"Teddy. Teddy, are you here?" Lydia asked in an overly serious tone. Nothing. We all looked at each other, giggling nervously.

"We aren't really expecting this to work, are we?" Ameera asked.

"Why else are we doing it?" Lydia answered.

A thump from upstairs made us all jump. As one, we lifted our hands off the tumbler and looked up at the ceiling.

"What was that?" Asked Ameera.

"Thought you said they were sleepin', Jo?" Sean said accusingly, giving me a dirty look.

"That's because they are sleeping." I snapped back at him. "Or at least they were. Maybe I should check again." But a feeling of fear had come over me, and I didn't want to climb those stairs again on my own.

"Are we doing this or not?" Ameera asked. "Cause if we don't do it soon, I'm going to lose my nerve."

"Um, everyone." Said Lydia in a small voice.

We all turned to look at her.

"Look!" She said, nodding at the board.

The glass was now over the 'Yes' on the board.

"Who moved it?" I asked, looking round the table. A murmur of 'not me' went round the group and everyone shook their heads.

"Sean?" I asked wearily.

"Wasn't me. Honest!" He exclaimed indignantly. "Musta been one of you three."

"Yes...what?" Ameera asked, leaning over the table to look closer at the glass, as if that would provide the answer.

"Yes...Teddy's here?" Lydia answered. "That's what I asked, wasn't it?"

"I think we should stop playing this." I said, feeling more fearful by the minute.

"We aren't 'playing' anything. It's not a toy!" Snapped Lydia. "It's a conduit to the other side and we should keep going."

"What if we don't like what's on the other side?" Ameera asked, sounding nervous now. She turned to me. "Joanna, be honest. Did you really see the shape of a man appear in Ada's bed?"

I looked at Ameera and then at Lydia and finally at Sean.

Say no. Say no and end this now before something bad happens. "Yes. I saw it," I answered truthfully, despite myself.

"Come on. Let's do this," said Lydia, reaching out to move the glass back to the middle of the board before resting her finger on top. Ameera and Sean obediently followed suit. But I couldn't summon the courage to lift my arm.

"It was you that interacted with it before, Jo. Come on, put your finger on it," Sean demanded.

Knowing I'd get no peace from Sean unless I did, reluctantly, I placed my finger on the edge of the tumbler.

"Now, ask it a question..." bossed Sean.

"Fine!" I hissed at him. "Teddy, if you're here..."

The tumbler flew across the Ouija Board under our fingers to the 'Yes.'

Everyone lifted their hands and jumped back in their seats, as if electrified. My stomach dropped. Something was here, with us.

"Who moved that?!" Sean shouted, accusingly. "This wasn't supposed to happen."

"I'm out," said Ameera.

"But we just got what we wanted!" Exclaimed Lydia. "It's communicating with us. Someone should ask more questions."

As we bickered around the table, some of us scared and some of us angry, the sound of the tumbler moving made us all look back down at the table.

The tumbler slowly moved itself over to the 'No.'

"Holy Shit!" Shouted Lydia.

Ameera started to cry. Sean looked fearfully around the room, as if an explanation would be found there.

Lydia stared at the board. "It must be very powerful if it can move objects on its own."

"Well, we knew that before tonight!" I said grumpily. "It moved the toys. It closed the door, and it hurt Ada. The board was supposed to help us communicate with it. But I don't think it wants to."

Sean leapt out of his seat, eyes wide with fear. "I thought you were lying!" He yelled at me, accusingly. "An' I thought that Ada was just a creepy little fucking weirdo! I was just doing this so I could get your mates round, spell out some fake ghost backstory shit and freak you all out!" Sean had turned purple with rage. "What the fuck is going on, Jo?!" He bellowed at me.

I lost it then and stood up from my seat. "*Ah, you are such a fucking dickhead, Sean!*" I roared back at him.

"Why are you all shouting?" Asked Ada.

Everyone jumped as none of us had noticed Ada coming into the room. I hadn't even heard the kitchen door.

"Why are you out of bed?!" I hissed at her, my heart pounding in my chest.

"Teddy woke me. He said to tell you to stop talking to him. He doesn't like it," she answered.

"Fuck sakes!" Sean said, running his hands over his head. "What else did he say?"

"He said I should go down and tell you to leave him alone. He's just here to talk to Ada, not you two, or to anyone else," Ada said calmly.

"Fuck this!" Sean said, striding to the kitchen door, clearly planning to storm out to the hall. "What the hell?" He gasped.

The door linking our kitchen and hallway was an old-fashioned type you don't see many of anymore. It had a wooden outer frame with a long glass insert. The glass was made of long, curved vertical stripes, designed to let light in but be opaque enough to give privacy. All of us looked out through the glass into the hallway. The dark silhouette of a child could be seen in front of the white PVC front door.

My fear kicked up a notch.

"Is that Nuala?" Ameera asked, still tearful.

"No, too short," I answered.

"I am so sick of this shit!" seethed Sean before yanking the door open.

"Don't!" I shouted.

But it was too late.

We all looked through the open doorway up the hall. It was empty.

"See!" yelled Sean. "It's just some trick of the light and all you fuckin' headers putting ideas in my head."

While Sean yelled at us, the door slammed shut on its own with a BANG, hard enough to make the glass vibrate.

We all jumped. No one spoke. Nervously, we all looked out to the hall again.

"What the fuck?" Sean uttered breathlessly. The dark outline of the child was back, about half-way down the hall this time.

This was no trick of the light.

Without speaking, we all began to move closer to each other and back up towards the back door.

"You're making him angry." said Ada in a singsong voice.

"Is that Teddy when he looks like a wee boy?" I breathed to Ada, with the blood pounding in my ears.

"Yes. Sometimes he's a boy, sometimes he isn't. He can look like anything. Make you see anything." Ada answered in a cheery tone.

I looked over at her. She was unusually perky for having just woken up.

“No, no, no. This isn’t fucking real,” said Sean. Angrily, he swung the door open again. The hallway was empty. “Where are you?!” He roared down the hallway.

“Calm down, Sean! And don’t close the door again,” I shouted at him.

“Oh, now you’re an expert? Why the fuck not?” Sean spat at me, gesturing wildly up the hall. “THERE’S NOTHING THERE!” He roared.

Just then, we heard the sound of footsteps on the stairs. They were light, childlike.

"Nuala?” I called. No answer.

The footsteps continued to descend. Sean and I looked at each other, both clearly worried about what Nuala might meet in the hall.

“Nuala, is that you?” I called again.

Still no answer.

“Something’s really wrong here” said Lydia. Sounding worried for the first time tonight.

The footsteps reached the hallway. My heart was in my throat as they reached the bottom step. Then, we all watched in horror, as a sleepy looking Ada stepped into the hallway.

"What are you all doing with Teddy?" Ada asked from the hall.

A low growl emanated from the direction 'Ada' had been.

The world shifted on its axis. My blood froze. I couldn't breathe. My legs almost buckled and my heart pounded.

Sean and I met eyes as we all slowly started to turn to where 'Ada' had been standing in the kitchen with us.

What we saw retained Ada's shape, more or less, but her auburn hair was now a matted, greasy black tangle and her face was gone, replaced by an animalistic, hide-skinned face-like shape with eyes as black as death looking back at us.

Around me, everyone started to cry and whimper, "Oh My God!" as terror overtook us. The creature in the kitchen started to shake unnaturally; a weird, hideous vibration like a bird's egg about to crack.

Suddenly, to our utter horror, it grew massively in height in a matter of seconds, towering over all of us.

Black eyes boring down at us, it opened its jaw and threw back its head.

The candles went out.

The creature let out a hideous screech.

All hell broke loose.

Cupboards and doors opened and closed. The floor vibrated and anything that wasn't nailed down was flung across the room. We lifted our arms to shield ourselves, each of us completely petrified.

"RUUUUNNNN!!" Yelled Sean, sprinting towards Ada and the front door. Lydia, Ameera and I ran to open the back door, clamouring and pushing past each other to get out first. The door wouldn't open. Ameera started screaming even louder as she frantically tried the handle.

I turned. The front door was now open, allowing light into the hall from the automatic porch light. The creature was walking out of the kitchen towards Ada in the hall, where she remained at the bottom of the stairs, watching it calmly.

Sean looked into the hall from the front garden. Upon seeing the creature come towards him, he slammed the front door shut, shutting Ada in with it and plunging us back into darkness.

"NOOO!" I screamed, fearing for Ada. Just then, the back door finally opened, and my friends dragged me out into the back garden. Screaming hysterically, we sprinted round the side of the house to the front driveway.

"Hello?"

As one, everyone screamed in poor Mum's face, making her scream too.

"What the hell is going on?" Demanded Dad. We all fell apart, crying and hugging for comfort. Sean and I tried to explain through our tears.

"Are you all blocked?" Was Mum's first question, as she tried to make sense of the three girls and one boy all babbling and crying in front of her. Frustrated and panicked herself, she asked, "Where's Ada now?"

Sean at least looked guilty.

I cried even harder. "She's still in there! With it!"

"Fuck sakes!" Mum muttered, shoving us out of the way before angrily striding up the path to the front door. She tried the handle, but it wouldn't turn. "Did you lock this?" She called to Sean, but she looked uncertain. She must have seen him running out of the house. Unless he'd stopped to put a key in the lock and turn it, he couldn't have locked the door. Sean just shook his head at her, a picture of guilt. I wanted to offer to go back in the house through the kitchen door, but I was still absolutely terrified, and my legs were like jelly.

"Right. I'll go round the back then, shall I?" Mum muttered, making to step off the porch.

At that moment, the door opened. Ada stood in the hallway, the picture of an angel with her auburn hair cascading down her shoulders, and a sad, stoic expression on her face.

Mum lifted her into her arms. “What happened, Sweetheart, you okay?” She asked her.

“Teddy left.” Ada said by way of an answer, hugging Mum tightly.

Sean and I looked warily at Ada. “How do we know you’re not Teddy?” I asked, hiding behind Sean.

“Shut up! You’re both in enough trouble.” Mum snapped at us. “Jesus, and there was me berating your father for not booking us into the restaurant on the right bloody day. It’s a good job we had to come straight back home again!”

“I told you. He’s gone for now. Says we’ll meet again later.” Ada said softly.

Mum gave Sean and I dirty looks. “Can’t get one bloody night out without a bloody drama.” She huffed as she climbed the stairs with Ada in her arms.

Dad came over to us. “I’ve had a word with those girls. They’re off home now. Bloody half-wits. Fake Ada my arse!” He grumbled, sounding thoroughly pissed off.

Sean and I warily entered the house behind Dad and kind of hovered in the hallway, unsure what to do next. We'd been scared out of our minds minutes ago, but now the house felt different. Empty.

"Oh, so this is how you scared the shit out of yourselves, is it? Eh?" Dad came out of the kitchen with the Ouija board in his hands. "Where'd ya get it?" He snapped, thrusting it at us.

"It's Lydia's," I answered.

"Feckin sure it is. She still seeing fairies or whatever up at the Funeral Home?" He shoved the board at me.

Reluctantly I took it from him. "It's called a Wake House."

"What? Whatever. Give this back to her in school next week and don't bring it here again. You're too chicken to play with it without scaring yourselves stupid. D'ya understand? Swear to God. Could you not just raid the drinks cabinet like normal teenagers?! And have you seen that state of the bloody kitchen! Get in there this minute and don't leave until it's absolutely spotless. This was supposed to be a treat for your Mum. She's not clearing up after you two morons."

Sean and I nodded. Now the moment has passed, it all felt surreal. From blind terror to sheepish apologies at breakneck speed.

Mum came downstairs on her own, with a face like thunder. "Nuala's still asleep. A miracle given the racket we came home to! And wee Ada's back in bed, delighted to be rid of Teddy, so she says. Well, I guess if he stays away, we can call the night a success, eh? And you two dim-witted fuckwits are grounded. For two weeks! D'ya hear me?!"

With that, she stomped off to the living room.

Sean and I looked at each other, too stunned to speak. "What the fuck just happened?" He asked, eventually.

"Buggered if I know." I answered honestly. "But I do think it's gone."

"Yeah." Sean said, looking around him. "I think you're right."

Chapter 15

The Gathering - 22:45

“And that was the tale of Teddy.” Joanna announces. “It was months before I stopped jumping at shadows and I couldn’t sleep with the light off until I moved out to go to uni. Honestly, if it wasn’t for Ameera and Lydia being there, I would doubt my story myself!”

"It was an awful experience.” Ameera agrees, downing the last of her wine. "We were lucky it didn’t hurt us.”

“Although I still don’t get why it left,” Lydia muses.

A companionable silence descends on the group. It seems like a truce has been formed now the night is ending, Sarah and LA having got over their tiff with Lydia. The mood is melancholic, wistful and nostalgic. Some of the group are still holding hands.

“We weren’t allowed back in your house for months after that, do you mind?” Says Ameera with a laugh. “Even now, I swear your Mum’s still frosty with me if I meet her out!”

“Your Dad was pure mean to me!” adds Lydia. “Thought I should’ve been sectioned for talking about spirits and entities and owning a Ouija Board.

Sure, you'd have been sent to Ada's Asylum years ago for less!"

"Ha! Very true." says LA. "No wonder the place was haunted; it was likely stuffed with perfectly sane women asking for a lawyer and a second opinion."

"And now we are the lawyers and doctors. How far we've come, eh ladies?" Sarah lifts her glass for all to cheers.

Pointedly, I keep my glass on the table, feeling it would be inappropriate for 'the cleaner' to join this particular toast. I haven't done much for equality in the workplace, have I?

Joanna gives Sarah a pointed look.

"Er, what did you think of the tales?" Ameera asks me with a bright smile, clearly sensing the tension.

"Yeah, they were great. Thanks for including me, everyone," I answer politely, looking round at everyone.

A chorus of 'oh you're welcome' and 'lovely to meet you' comes from the group. But an awkward atmosphere remains.

"Ach, poor wee Ada," says Eleanor, thickly. "An' her with all her problems now. It's not fair. Do you remember what a beauty she was? Like something out of a fairytale." She turns to Joanna. "D'you think she'll be okay?"

Joanna hesitates. "Yes, she's a fighter. We're doing everything we can for her. No stone left unturned."

A look passes between Joanna, Sarah and Ameera. They nod to each other. I wonder if Sarah is part of Ada's care team. No, she works in the maternity ward, that isn't likely. Maybe Ameera?

"Tell her I was askin' for her, won't ya?" Eleanor slurs before burping loudly. Sarah tuts at her and starts gathering up the glasses and carrying them to the dishwasher. Everyone takes the hint and starts gathering their belongings.

Finally! The party is over. I carry my dishes over and start to give Joanna a hand with the dishwasher.

Joanna squeezes my arm. "Thanks. Don't rush off. As I said earlier, Ameera is going your way and will give you a lift home now."

"Oh, there's no need. I could do with the walk to the bus stop to sober me up." I reply, slurring slightly. "It's late. You're taking that lift." Joanna replies, in a tone that brooked no argument. *Fine by me,* I think, remembering the rain while looking round for my coat.

I can't say I've enjoyed the evening exactly, but it has certainly been memorable. And the food has been outstanding. Joanna appears with coats from the utility room, and we all shuffle down the hall to the front door.

Whereas the kitchen area is cosy, the hall has a real chill. I remember the growl with a shiver. Maybe Joanna is minding a pet for someone. I still feel irked by her dismissiveness. I should have pressed her for an answer.

"Jeez, radiators broke out here Jo?" Asks Lydia, subtle as ever.

"No point heating the whole house, eh?" Joanna answers sounding frazzled.

"Sure you don' need any help gettin' cleared up d'ya, love?" Slurs Eleanor.

"Sarah is staying to help. You jump into the taxi with LA and Lydia. You'll be glad to see your bed tonight." Joanna tells her, ushering us all out the door.

The women are warmer with me than they had been earlier in the evening, saying they hope I'll come to the next one and pulling me into drunken hugs. I follow Ameera to her car and gratefully jump in.

It is only when Ameera pulls away from the kerb that it occurs to me - hasn't she been drinking too? She is a GP for goodness sake! I hope she won't be stopped by the police on the way home while I'm in the car. I need to get home.

"Dammit!" She exclaims, making me jump.

"What's wrong?" I ask.

"Forgot my phone," she answers, indicating and turning left down a side street to head back the way we came.

Ah for God's sake, is this night never going to end? I'd be quicker bloody walking.

She pulls up on the pavement around the corner from Joanna's. "Would you mind running in to get it for me?" Ameera asks.

Seriously? Where do these women get off? Well, I guess she is doing me a favour. Supressing a sigh, I jump out of the car and jog up to Joanna's side door that leads to the utility room.

She opens the door a second after I knock, making me jump. "Yes?" She asks, a slightly manic smile on her face.

I wonder if I've caught her in the middle of something she doesn't want me to see. "Um, Sorry. Ameera forgot her phone. Have you seen it?"

“Come in! We’ll have a look together.” She half yells, grabbing my arm and wrenching me through the door. I go back into the kitchen. Sarah is sitting at the table with a serious look on her face. A small Nokia is in the centre of the table.

“Maybe that’s it?” Joanna asks loudly, pointing to it.

“Um, probably.” I say, wondering why she is being so weird. I note that Sarah doesn’t offer to bring the phone to me. Sure, I’m just the cleaner.

Really irritated now, I walk to the table and snatch up the phone. Behind me, I hear the door from the kitchen to the utility room close. I turn to see that Ameera has just come in.

“Is this it?” I ask, waving the phone in the air. She doesn’t reply.

Ameera and Joanna step towards me. Involuntarily, I take a step back.

“Ow!” I yell. Looking down, I see Sarah taking a needle out of my arm.

“Wha’ did you do?” I ask in a thick voice.

Sarah, Ameera and Joanna move to form a semi-circle around me.

“I’m so sorry,” says Joanna.

I flail out to push Sarah, but my arm won't work properly. What has she injected me with? What is happening? I try to speak but can't form the words. My heart races and the world tilts.

As I fall, the women reach out to catch me.

The three women half carry, half drag me over to the sofa and lay me out on it. I can just see Joanna and Ameera leave the room from the corner of my eye and hear them go up the stairs.

Sarah sits beside me on the sofa, looking at me sadly. She gently pulls the hair off my face. "This'll all be over soon," she says in a low voice. Then she pulls on a chain at her neck, tugging a small crucifix out of her top. She kisses it before placing it back under her top again, patting it over her heart.

I try to speak, to beg her for help, but I can't make a sound. Sarah stands up and leaves me. I hear the French doors open and shut and see that the outside light has come on. Straining to see, I watch the living room door, waiting for Ameera and Joanna to return.

Noises float down from upstairs. Sounds of a struggle. Growls and snarls. Panic sets in as my body tries to counter whatever they've poisoned me with to subdue me. Tears flow down my temples. I can barely wiggle my fingers.

After a few minutes, Sarah and Ameera step through the door, dragging something that is fighting to free itself.

Oh my God, who the hell is that?!

Frozen, I watch in horror as they drag the snarling, skeletal form into the room. Dressed in a dirty straitjacket, it fights, bites and kicks at the women. I can see it has a sturdy metal collar around its neck and dirty auburn hair over its face. Joanna holds the end of the chain attached to the collar, dragging it forward. Ameera pushes it from behind. Both women are struggling, despite how tiny the figure is.

"Get it down on the floor beside her," Joanna shouts to Ameera, over the commotion.

They force it down beside me on the floor and the stench of rot, shit and decay fills my nostrils. Ameera straddles over it while Joanna tries to pin down its head. Its hair falls back and I can see the mad, ruined face of a woman who has long lost all reason.

Total terror floods me. What is going to happen next?

"Has she got the defib ready?" Ameera shouts.

Joanna turns to look out to the back garden, to where Sarah has gone.

"Yes! Do it! Now!!" Joanna shouts over the spitting and hissing.

Ameera has another injection ready. It takes the women a few moments to get the crazed woman beneath them still enough to inject her, while she growls, snaps and snarls like a wounded hyena. They almost don't manage it.

When Ameera eventually gets the needle in, the tiny, madwoman arches up unnaturally, shaking both women off of her. They jump up from the floor and dart away.

Come back! Please don't leave me here, I beg silently, scared beyond reason.

I hear the French doors open and close. The key turns in the lock.

It is just us in the room.

I fear I will have a heart attack, so great is my terror. I hear the thing on the ground writhing and howling in obvious pain.

It lets out a few sharp breaths, before going still. Too still.

I clamp my eyes shut. I feel the sofa depress beside me, as if someone has sat down next to me. I can't open my eyes. I cry and think of my family.

Something cold touches my arms and face, probing gently at first, then more urgently.

I feel something enter my ear, then my mouth, and my nose.

I retch and shake.

There is an enormous pressure on my chest.

I am certain I am dying.

In my last moments before everything goes black, I hear the doors open and the women rush back in, barking orders, urgently swinging into action.

But they aren't rushing to help me.

Epilogue

Exhausted, I reach a hand up to wipe away the tears on my cheek. I've been so immersed in my memories, it's almost a shock to bring the room back into focus. The uncomfortable chair. The cloying smell of the cleaning products. The too-bright lights.

I look over and see the Doctor is also crying softly. We hold our gaze for a long moment. She looks away first and begins to cry in earnest.

"How could you do it to me, Joanna?" I ask her.

Her face crumples with guilt and her voice cracks. "I'm so sorry. You have to believe me. She was my little sister. She had two wee kids who needed her. I had to help her."

"I had a kid who needed me!" I snap back at her.

"I know!" She wails, hiding her head in her hands. "I know *now*. But I didn't know until afterwards, when it was too late. You never told me you had a son!"

"I didn't want you to know! You'd have pitied us, me as a single mam, him for the shitty secondary school he went to. You'd have foisted your family's ugly hand-me-down M&S clothes on to us, trying to help us out. We didn't need your charity! Or your patronising pity!"

"I am so sorry. Genuinely I am. It was a terrible thing to do. And I've had to live with the guilt all these years." She gulps, trying to calm herself.

Her self-pity fuels my hatred like petrol on a bonfire. My eyes wander to the photo on her desk. In it, Joanna is surrounded by the women from that night, taken years later, celebrating someone's birthday. With them is Ada, beaming and radiant, completely unrecognisable from the pitiful wretch I'd seen that night. Another picture shows Joanna smiling with her grandchildren, twin girls and an older boy.

"Tell me again how it happened." I demand.

"No! I can't tell it again. This has been hard enough. And it's late! Please Muireann."

"Oh, *now* you can pronounce my name! Good of you to learn it at last!" I snap at her.

She looks wretched. I have no sympathy. Moments pass. I'm in no hurry. Joanna glances towards the door.

Don't call the orderlies. Not. Just. Yet.

"Very well, you deserve that." She begins, in a thin voice. Relief floods me. Thankfully, Joanna loves the sound of her own voice and, after hearing me paint her in such a bad light, I knew she'd be vain enough to want to tell her side of the story.

Let's hear it, bitch.

"It started shortly after Ada returned home from Connemara and her role at the Asylum. The first few weeks were fine. We listened to her experience at the Asylum in astonishment and, frankly, disbelief. We watched as she searched for a new job to rebuild her life. But after a few weeks, it became apparent something was very, very wrong with her."

"She'd say terrible things. She stopped caring for her children, physically and emotionally. We thought she had depression, or post-traumatic stress. We couldn't fully believe her story from the Asylum, but it was clear that *something* bad had happened and had really affected her. We got help for her, but she didn't respond to treatment. No medicine helped. She got progressively sicker, and her behaviour became worse and worse."

"Within weeks she'd swear, kick, bite and slap anyone around her without provocation, our parents included. We couldn't leave her alone with her children, or she'd hurt them. We all helped as best we could and delayed the inevitable for as long as we could. But it wasn't sustainable. Three months after returning from the Asylum, Ada was sectioned, a shadow of the women she'd been. She came here," Joanna gestures around her to the secure mental hospital that had been my home for over twenty years, "where we did everything to help her."

Joanna pauses to wipe her eyes and take a sip of water. Her eyes are unfocussed as she continues, clearly still feeling the pain of those dark days.

"As the months passed and nothing worked, the conversation around her treatment started to change. Nothing added up. Sedatives that could've felled a bull had no effect. Her muscles were wasted and withered, and she weighed less than six stone, but it took three orderlies to overpower her. Those around her started to experience things they couldn't explain. Noises. Voices. Horrendous nightmares. Dark urges. No one could explain it. She was all anyone talked about on the wards. I hadn't told anyone Ada's story of Patient A in the Asylum. I didn't want to sound unprofessional, but I started to wonder if what she'd said was true. And if so, what could that mean?"

"While I dithered, paralysed by indecision, out of the blue the priest from the Asylum called to my parents' house to ask after Ada. They were her emergency contacts, he explained. He had tried to contact Ada many times after she'd fled, without success. He'd just received curt texts saying she was fine and not to contact her again, but he couldn't stop worrying about her. He listened as my parents told him about her deterioration. When he heard her sister was part of her care team, he asked to speak to me. I'll never forget his kindness in not telling my parents what he suspected. We met at my parents' house and spoke alone. With a heavy heart he told me the story of Patient A."

"Her name was Helen O'Connell. She'd been a successful B&B owner who'd rarely ever left Connemara. A well-known and popular member of her community, she had three children and a husband who adored her. Without explanation, sometime in her early thirties, she started behaving erratically; becoming violent and abusive to those around her. Doctors and consultants treated her for months, ruling out a brain tumour, Tourette's and schizophrenia. But Helen's behaviour worsened until there was no alternative but to commit her. At the Asylum, the doctors tried everything they could think of using conventional medicine, without any success. Helen's condition continued to deteriorate until they feared she would die. Then, things started to happen that couldn't be explained. Staff and patients were adversely affected by proximity to her."

"The old psychiatrist was the first to connect the dots, partly because he'd heard old stories of patients believed to be possessed, but mostly because of what he personally experienced with her. When he was alone with her, she'd terrified him by wearing his wife's face and recounting terrible things, all of which she couldn't possibly know. She'd speak of how his father was a violent drunk. And she didn't speak in general terms, it wasn't guesswork. No, she'd recount violent episodes he'd only confided to his wife."

"Like when he was eight and his father learned his mother was pregnant again. He flew into a rage, accused her of infidelity, and beat her until she miscarried, right there in front of him and his young siblings. When the ambulance took her away, his father told the kids to tell the Guards she'd fallen down the stairs. No one outside of his family knew that story. No one knew he still had nightmares, during which he watched his father punch and kick his mother in the stomach, calling her a whore as the blood flowed between her legs. Only his wife knew. And his wife had been dead for years. That was when the psychiatrist called the church for help."

"We're not particularly open to tales of possession," the priest told me, "despite what the movies would have you believe." Belief in it was rare amongst priests. He himself had dismissed it, until Helen. He arrived at the Asylum adamant the old psychiatrist had a mad woman on his hands but it wasn't long before he changed his mind."

"He wouldn't tell me what he saw, only that it still haunted him. Anyway, it was sufficient to convince him that the old psychiatrist was telling the truth and in need of help."

"The priest sought all the advice he could get and dragged in experts from Europe. Demonic possession was confirmed, and exorcisms were performed. Many of them. Nothing worked. Out of respect, they renamed her Patient A as Helen would never have done or said what the thing in her body said and did. They focussed their efforts on how to control and contain the demon. They isolated Patient A and minimised her contact with anyone. The isolation seemed to settle the demon. Or, that's what it wanted them to think. It ate and drank just enough to keep Helen's body alive, in a state akin to hibernation."

"The priest communicated with it from time to time, trying to determine which demon it was. It called itself 'The Devourer', amongst other names, which didn't correlate to any known demons. That was no surprise, of course, as demons aren't known for their honesty. The years passed. Ridiculous as it sounds, they started to get blasé around it. Bored by the repetitive weekly cleanings and blessings. But The Devourer was playing the long game. Lulling them into a false sense of security while waiting for an opportunity. They were sloppy with Ada. He could see that now."

"After the 'incident' with my sister, Patient A stopped eating altogether. What happens to demons when their host body dies is, apparently, the subject of much debate in the church. The priest said that's just the church's way of saying 'no one knows.' With the demon inside her, it still took more than a month for her to die. During that time, they believe it was transitioning to Ada, getting stronger in the new host while waiting for the old one to die."

"The priest spoke to Patient A's husband a few times towards the end as they kept him informed of her deterioration. Her husband knew the truth, though her children did not. The priest asked him again about when it had started. Her husband couldn't pinpoint any big event or cause at the time."

"When asked if anything unusual had happened in the weeks and months *before* his wife first became sick, all he could think of was that a resident in the B&B had checked in a few months ago for a week and died during their stay. He'd been an odd, cantankerous man in his late sixties. He wouldn't say where he was from and once he checked in, he didn't leave the B&B. They worried he'd been recently let out of prison. When he didn't come down for breakfast one day, they forced their way into his room and found him dead in the bed."

"It transpired that he was a loner and hoarder from about fifty miles away. Helen and her husband reckoned he came to their B&B so he wouldn't die alone and felt bad for thinking ill of him."

"A few months later, Helen's behaviour was so unpredictable and out of character, her husband went to the GP for help. Four months after that, she was committed permanently. The priest couldn't be sure, but he theorised that the demon travelled in the man to find a new host and poor Helen was who he found. He didn't know why it chose Ada as its next host. Maybe just because she was the first to let her guard down, when Helen's body was failing."

"It was so much to take in. I wanted to believe the priest, and it all added up. But it was just too fantastical. I was a medical professional who worked with some of the most criminally insane in Ireland. I had no shortage of patients declaring 'The Devil made me do it!'"

"But then I'd remembered Teddy and the night of the Ouija board. Hadn't I already witnessed the unexplainable around Ada? Maybe I just didn't want it to be true."

"The priest knew by my face that I was conflicted. He asked me to keep him updated and call him if I needed help. The main thing, he beseeched me, was to keep Ada away from others if she appeared to be nearing the end of her life."

“What should I do in that scenario? I asked him. Call him was his answer. But in my heart, I knew he had no solutions. Only prayers and debated theories. He left, promising to keep in touch.”

“Weeks passed and Ada got sicker. Those around her became affected more and more horribly. I was desperate. I loved her so much and it ripped the heart from my chest every time her children and my parents asked for updates on her.” Joanna pauses, sobbing so hard her shoulders shake.

I wait for her to compose herself.

“And then?” I press.

“Pleease Muireann! I can’t.” She wails.

“You can. You did. Go on.” I feel completely calm, as we near the end.

Joanna pulls in deep shuddery breaths.

“And then, I formed a plan. I theorised, if ‘The Devourer’ had to leave the body upon death, what if I killed Ada, then resuscitated her minutes later?” Joanna stares at me, beseeching me to let her stop. “Maybe I could save her.”

I coolly meet her gaze. “And what did you need for this plan to work?”

Joanna squeaks, utterly distraught as she revisits the truth of what she did.

"Well?"

"A new host."

"And who did you know, that wouldn't be missed?" I ask, lightly.

She gives a cry of anguish, tears streaming down her face. Her hands cover her mouth, trying to keep the truth in.

"But you couldn't do it alone, could you?" I continue. "You're a medical professional, not a doctor. I always thought you were a Life Coach who helped middle-aged people through midlife crises."

"Hardly anyone knows what an Occupational Therapist is. And as I work with the criminally insane. It's best not to let too many people know where I work and what I do. 'Life Coach' was an easy cover."

"And you don't go by your married name, McCann, here, do you?"

"No, I go by my maiden name, Neilly. Most women with PhDs do. It's expensive and fiddly to change the name you got your Doctorate with," she explains.

I nod in mock sympathy. "Ah. I understand. And then all you had to do was convince Ameera and Sarah to help you. It took me a while to figure that part out. They're both family, aren't they?"

"Yes. Ameera is married to Sean and Sarah's my cousin. I told them the story the priest told me, and I brought them to see her. It took some convincing, but they came around eventually. Ameera had been there the night we saw Teddy. And they'd had their own experiences with the...unexplainable. They know there's more to this world than what we see. And, crucially, Ada was dying. So, when I begged and begged them to help me, they could see the affect her illness was having on her kids and my parents. They wanted to help her."

"How did you get Ada out of here?" I ask. "It's like Fort bloody Knox."

"Sarah and Ameera helped me fake papers to transfer her to The Royal Victoria Hospital in Belfast for treatment. I offered to help transport her in the ambulance. It was planned for the evening, so we wouldn't upset visitors at the hospital and Ada was heavily sedated. When the orderlies and I arrived at the hospital, Sarah and Ameera met us for the handover. Then we took her out a side entrance and drove her here. As Sarah and Ameera are both doctors, it was easy enough to pull off."

"I bet. Everyone trusts well educated, middle-class white women, don't they? That's what makes them so fucking dangerous. Did Ameera and Sarah take much convincing about my role in the plan?"

"We all did. Honest. We figured, worst case scenario, there was no demon, the sedative would wear off and you'd be fine. We'd say you were drunk and deny drugging you."

"That was the worst-case scenario?" I scoff.

"No! For us. Not for you. Obviously, the worst-case scenario was that the demon was real, and it left her body and entered yours."

"Worst case scenario for me, not for you. Your worst case scenario was that it didn't work. In that scenario, I'd wake up from the sedative and accuse you three of drugging me and leaving me unable to move in a room with a mad woman. That's why we all had to endure that Godawful Gathering. If it all went to shit, you'd say I was drunk and delirious after a night of ghost stories. Who the hell would believe the word of a poverty line cleaner over a bunch of overachieving pillars of the community."

"Yes! No! No! It was awful. Truly awful. I can honestly say none of us really thought it was going to be successful."

"But if it was successful, dispensable me would face the consequences. Not you three."

"Yes." Joanna answers in a small voice, defeated.

We stare at each other across the room, the wickedness and enormity of Joanna's actions laid bare. She can't justify herself anymore.

"My memories were patchy for so long, Joanna. But when that new doctor you don't like overruled you and started me on a new treatment, I saw an opportunity. I had long stopped fighting the beast and bargained and bartered with it instead. Pretend the medicine works, I begged, and I'll get you access to more people. More freedom. Oh, he's a wily aul bastard. He retreated, diminished himself. He watched and waited. He let me remember. It should have brought joy, not anguish. Like remembering the day the staff brought a handsome man in to see me. A man who called me 'Mam.' A man I'd no memories of at all, unfortunately."

I pause and close my eyes to quell the rage building within. The rage fuels the demon within, and I feel it stir with anticipation.

"Why was I brought here, Joanna?" My voice is ice cold now.

Joanna covers her eyes.

"Joanna..." I singsong.

"No! Please Muireann!! I can't!"

“You can. You did. Tell me. Why was I committed here?” Hot anger rushes through me. The Devourer thrums.

“A couple of weeks after that evening, you burned your son’s fingers with straightening irons. The neighbours heard the screams. You were arrested that night and sectioned after a few weeks of evaluation.”

“That seems extreme. I’m guessing that’s not the first time I’d hurt him?”

“No. He had...” Joanna pauses, looking wretched. “He had many injuries.”

My poor son. Rage burns and The Devourer flexes and purrs within me.

Nearly there. Just wait.

“You put a demon in me and just...dropped me home?”

“I thought you lived alone. I swear!”

“But still. You just...left me?”

“We assumed it would be weeks before it would take effect, like with Ada. The plan was to check in on you after a few weeks.”

“But?”

“But you were sectioned before I had the chance to see if you were okay.”

Sectioned and forever labelled a deranged and abusive mother.

The demon's hackles raise.

"I wonder why Joanna? Perhaps The Devourer was starved of playthings, all those years locked inside incarcerated Helen and then Ada, unable to hurt anyone. It must have been delighted to find a skinny, lonely kid waiting for it. Or maybe you hadn't a clue what would happen and were messing with things you had no understanding of at all! There was no slow transition with me, it just slid right in and took over straight away!"

We pause for a moment, both breathing heavily with the exhaustion of remembering.

"What was his name?" I ask.

Joanna looks at me, tears streaming.

"My son, Joanna. What was his name?"

"Fintan." She answers in a low tone. She swallows, before continuing. "I am truly, truly, sorry, Muireann. I'd do anything to have done things differently."

Fuck you, Joanna!

Fuck your apology!

The Devourer prepares to pounce.

Wait!

"I don't think you're sorry at all, Joanna. You may feel guilty, but *you* got your sister back. *You* faced The Devourer and won. Not me. I lost my life. My shitty little tower block life that didn't hold a candle to your fucking fairy lights life!"

"And you've been calculating, keeping me hidden here. You've kept me drugged. You've been my occupational therapist. You've treated me alone, so no one could hear me if I started raving about you and what you did! You planned that whole 'Gathering' so you had witnesses to say I'd left with Ameera, fit and well so no one would believe me if I told them what happened. That's when I can speak at all. You've even fought against me getting better treatment and, you haven't even isolated me! No priest visits here! I can feel The Devourer roaming the corridors at night, feeding off the poor bastards around me. Sure, they're all criminally insane. No need to protect them!"

"I am a good person. I help people!" Joanna says, resolutely, banging her fist on the arm of her chair like a belligerent child.

"No. You think you are. But you're a fucking cunt, Joanna." I spit at her.

The Devourer laughs and coils itself, ready to spring.

"Right! This has gone far enough. I'm sorry, I really am. It's late and I need to get home."

"I'm sorry too, Joanna. I really am." I mock, with acid sweetness.

With unexpected speed and agility, I leap off my seat, fly across the room and wrestle Joanna to the floor. She shrieks and fights, but I clamp my hand in her mouth, letting her bite down on my hand. Normally, I'm weak, drugged, wasted and withered. Barely seven stone.

But twenty years is a long time to get to know the beast within you.

I'd started to bargain with The Devourer years ago when the new treatment started.

I'll get you a new body. A free one! On the outside of these walls. You just need to behave. Be still. Be quiet. Be patient. Get them to lower their guard around me. Make me appear unthreatening. Get us in front of HER. Then, when the moment is right, give me the strength to strike!

With my free hand, I grab Joanna's hair, still highlighted blonde despite her age. I bang and bang and bang her head off the floor, fuelled by hatred. Blood blooms beneath her. The Devourer rejoices in the metallic tang of the blood and urges me to keep going.

No! That's not the plan.

The Devourer and I stand up. Joanna gurgles and moans beneath me on the floor, hands rising to her head. Blood pools underneath her. Resolutely, I walk over to her handbag. The Devourer pulses and vibrates with pleasure and excitement within me.

Patience my old friend, I sooth it. *Soon, we will both be free.*

I reach into Joanna's handbag, feeling for her trademark silk head scarf. Scarves aren't allowed in wards for the criminally insane, of course. But rules don't apply to the Joanna's of the world. I'd heard the orderlies moan about how she never follows policy or protocol and never gets pulled up for it, while they get criticised for every small misstep.

I pull out a bright pink and navy silk scarf with a beautifully ornate Chinese print. It is a perfect match for her pink shift dress. Of course it fucking is.

Hooks aren't allowed on doors in asylums either, but The Devourer had convinced an inmate to take his own life a while ago and we'd learned a trick from them, only they'd used a strip of bed sheet.

I tie a knot in one end of the scarf and open the door a crack to look outside. We've spoken late into the evening and the corridor is quiet. They've probably forgotten about us. I swing the scarf over the top of the door, closing the door and catching the knot on the outside. I tug on the scarf, feeling its resistance. It will do just fine.

Turning to face Joanna, I wrap the rest of the scarf around my neck, like I've practised in my mind for months. All I need to do is lean forward and let gravity do the work.

Joanna rouses herself from the ground just then, pulling herself up on shaking arms. She looks up at me in horror when it dawns on her what is going to happen.

"No! Please Muireann! Don't! The twins are staying with us! It's not safe! PLEASE!!" She begs.

I smile at her across the room.

"I am truly, truly sorry, Joanna." I lie, smiling.

Pressing my feet to the door, I push myself forward and almost immediately feel the light begin to fade.

I say a fond goodbye to my dark companion as I feel it ease itself from my body, eager to begin again.

A feeling of peace washes over me, like a warm wave on a sunny beach.

Suddenly, it's just me again.

Not the cleaner.

Not the abusive Mum whose son was taken into care.

Just Muireann.

As Joanna's screams fade into the distance, I welcome the silence and the peace it brings.

Acknowledgements

I would like to acknowledge my editor, June Russell-Alexander, without whose guidance this book wouldn't exist. A true champion for new, female writers, June shaped this book from a rough draft to something I'm proud to publish. I literally couldn't have done it without you, June.

What's that expression, 'Good friends lend an ear, great friends help you bury the bodies..?' I have to thank the family and friends who, when told I was writing a book, offered nothing but encouragement, allowing me to hold the imposter syndrome at bay long enough to finish it. To Emma, Suzanne, Rachael, Mairead, Joanne and Susan, I give heartfelt thanks.

Lastly, thank you to my husband, Niall and sons, Drew and Eddie. Thank you for your patience while I hid myself away to write. I love you all.

About the Author

Ruth S Cunningham lives in a house with a yellow door, in South Belfast, the city she was born and raised in, with her husband, two teenage boys, two dogs and a very grumpy tortoise.

Describing herself as a 'horror obsessive,' she consumes horror novels, podcasts, films and TV shows every chance she gets.

This is her debut novel.

A Small Favour with a Big Impact

If you enjoyed this book, please consider leaving a review on Amazon and Goodreads.

Your feedback not only supports the author but also helps other readers discover their work.

Even a few words can make a big difference.

Thank you for being part of this author's writing journey.

Russell-Alexander Publishing

Printed in Dunstable, United Kingdom

77416139R00184